BETRAYED
POWELL BOOK 4

Bill Ward

Copyright © 2016 Bill Ward
All rights reserved.
ISBN-13:
978-1533561732
ISBN-10:
1533561737

I would like to mention Emma, Rebecca, Ben, Chloe, Natasha, Alexandra, Cassandra, Victoria and Danny. An amazing and varied collection of children! I love you all.

I also wish to say a huge Thanks to Jel for all of my cover designs. A fantastically gifted designer, who interprets my very brief notes and delivers amazing covers!

CHAPTER ONE

Fear gripped every cell in his body. He now knew the terror of being hunted. Was this how the fox felt when pursued by a pack of dogs? He could hear them approaching and was regretting his decision not to keep running.

He had been out of breath and his legs were turning to jelly when he decided to hide in the clump of bushes. He had hoped they would give up searching and then he could make his escape. So far that was proving to be a flawed plan.

Although he couldn't risk moving his body, his brain was hyper active. Right now, he was regretting more than just choosing to hide and not flee. Top of the list was the decision not to join two of his friends in training to run the Brighton marathon but sport had never held any fascination. For the twenty eight years of his life so far, he had avoided all forms of physical exercise.

He had been fooled into thinking it was unnecessary as he ate healthily and his weight hadn't changed much since he was a teenager. Why didn't someone point out to him, he might one day have to outrun two men both intent on doing him serious harm.

Other regrets were coming thick and fast. He wished he'd never decided to study journalism. Even more, he wished he hadn't then decided to investigate the people living in this country house. Hell, even though he called himself a reporter, he didn't actually have a job since being let go by the local newspaper. They had budget cuts and applied the rule, he was the last to join so would be the first let go.

Most of the other reporters were dinosaurs not long away from collecting their pensions. He had wanted to prove the paper had made a terrible mistake, by breaking a big story on the front pages of a national newspaper, not just some local rag. Now he feared the only way he would make it onto the front pages would be as a headline announcing his death.

Perhaps he was over reacting? He needed to get a grip. He wasn't Bob Woodward and this wasn't another Watergate. Scott Rivers wasn't Nixon. He was just another manipulative son of a bitch brainwashing and exploiting lost souls in search of something new.

The truth was, he had been fed up of working for a local paper but didn't appreciate the paper deciding when he should leave. He had ambition and wanted to be working in London on a national daily not be buried away in West Sussex.

Now his ambition had led to him desperately hugging the ground with his heart beating so fast, he thought it would explode. He was more than just scared, he was terrified.

He could hear their footsteps crushing the leaves and twigs as the two men came closer. They were walking slowly, obviously searching the trees and bushes for any sign of him.

"He definitely ran in this direction," the man he knew as Roger said to his companion.

"Stuart," the other man called out. His name was Tommy and he was Scott's right hand man. Living at the house, you quickly learned Tommy was a man who didn't expect to ask twice when he wanted something done. "Come out here and we can all get back in the warm," Tommy encouraged. "Scott just wants to talk to you. He's very disappointed by your attitude. He wants to understand better why you want to leave. And if you still want to leave after a further conversation, you can go without any problem. We just need to get you to sign a confidentiality agreement." Tommy sounded very reasonable and it made him even more menacing than usual. Stuart knew for certain Tommy was not a reasonable man.

Stuart was tempted to put an end to matters by standing up but he couldn't sign any agreement, he wouldn't then be able to publish his story. That would mean everything he'd gone through was for nothing.

At least they didn't know he was a journalist. They just thought he was unhappy with Scott's teachings and wanted to leave. When he'd said as much to Scott, it had resulted in him being locked in his room, despite his protests. They treated him like a naughty child. He was allowed out for breakfast and that was when he sneaked out through the toilet window and made a run for the woods.

"Stuart, if you don't come out here, I'm going to get pretty pissed off," Tommy warned. "I haven't finished my breakfast."

Stuart was getting extremely uncomfortable where he was hiding. The grass was damp and the morning dew was seeping through his clothes. It was April and so far proving to be a very wet Spring. He desperately wanted to stretch his limbs. Instead, he held his breath and didn't risk moving a muscle. The woods were extensive and eventually surely they must go search elsewhere.

"He's not here," a disgruntled Tommy said, after a minute. "We're wasting our time. Let's go."

Stuart sighed with relief as he realised they were leaving. He didn't dare move for several more minutes but he could detect no hint of danger. There was only silence in the woods, interrupted by the occasional sound of birds flitting about in the branches of the trees overhead.

He slowly raised his head to check the situation. There was no sign of anyone and he climbed to his feet, shaking the leaves from his clothes and stretching his muscles. He allowed himself a small smile and believed for the first time he might actually be able to escape. Brain defeats brawn...

"I guess Roger was right after all," Tommy said, emerging from behind a tree and interrupting Stuart's thoughts.

Stuart was frozen to the spot for a second. His brief moment of joy quickly dissolved in a wave of panic.

"Come and speak with Scott," Tommy encouraged, taking a few steps nearer. "I don't get why you're acting so strange. Scott likes you." They were now about twenty metres apart.

Stuart instinctively turned and ran away from the danger Tommy presented. He knew it was hopeless. Tommy was fit and athletic. Stuart spent most of his time sitting behind a desk exercising his fingers on a keyboard. Sheer desperation kept him in front for a while but he could hear Tommy gaining ground.

Stuart was running around the edge of the high wall, which circled the house and grounds. No wonder the house was called Tintagel. It was like a bloody castle! According to legend, Tintagel was supposedly where King Arthur was born. Scott thought of himself as King Arthur but actually he was more in the mould of Merlin, weaving spells over his followers.

Stuart couldn't hope to climb over the massive wall, which must be at least fifteen feet high. He would soon be at the main gate but it would be locked and there was no hope of escape. Adrenaline had kept him going further than he would have thought possible but his legs were once again hurting with the effort of running and he had to stop or he would shortly collapse.

He came to a halt and bent over double, trying to catch his breath. He turned back to face Tommy, who was now walking toward him, showing no signs of being out of breath. It was never an equal match but the bastard was laughing at his pitiful attempt to escape.

"I don't want to speak to Scott," Stuart said defiantly. "I just want to leave."

"You need to get fitter," Tommy answered with a smile. "We're going back to the house. You lead the way."

There was a large tree branch on the ground and Stuart thought about picking it up as a weapon but decided against. He had no doubt Tommy could beat him senseless if it came to a fight. Better not to provoke him.

He started walking towards the house without further argument. He felt defeated and there was nothing else to say.

CHAPTER TWO

Powell arrived a couple of minutes early at the house in Putney. He knew it was becoming a bit of an old fashioned concept but he couldn't imagine turning up late for a meeting. Too often, he found younger people in particular would send a message saying they were running late. Brought up in a time when there were no mobile phones, you made sure you allowed time for unforeseen circumstances and arrived early if there were no delays. Powell considered being punctual a sign of respect for the person you are meeting. He showed the same respect to everyone but especially for a potential new client.

He had a minimum amount of background from his telephone conversation with Clara Buckingham but she had almost begged him to meet. She had been referred to him by Angela Bennett, who he had helped recover her children from Saudi Arabia. Powell had stressed he could not return to Saudi, where if he was arrested, the best result might see him languishing in a jail for a very long time. It was better not to ponder the other possible outcomes of returning to a country where they did not treat kindly, foreigners who broke their laws and Powell had broken them in abundance.

The upmarket sounding Clara had confirmed that the help she needed wouldn't require him to leave the country and thus he had accepted the invitation to her home. He had looked her up on the internet and discovered she was married to a Charles Buckingham and they definitely belonged in the super rich club. Even the name shouted privilege and old money. They both came from wealthy families so there was no hint of Clara having married into money. She seemed to be best known for helping various charities while he was a stockbroker.

Powell thought it a little odd it had been the wife who made the call. There was possibly some significance in Charles's reluctance to initiate first contact. Perhaps he didn't believe his daughter was in as much trouble as Clara had suggested. Or maybe he didn't like to air the dirty, family laundry in public.

A maid opened the door, introduced herself as Rosa, and showed Powell into the living room, confirming he was expected. Rosa promised Mr. and Mrs. Buckingham would be with him shortly. He accepted the offer of coffee and took a seat on the cream, striped sofa.

He glanced back to check his feet hadn't left any dirty footmarks on the beige carpet. He felt like he was in a show home for a very exclusive development. There were few signs a family actually lived in the room. Perhaps that was down to Rosa's diligent work. He found himself wondering if they also had a butler. He'd never met a real life butler, only seen them in films.

Powell was intrigued why anyone with so much wealth would want his services. Why was he a better option than the police or courts? Not that he was complaining. He had been pleased to receive the call requesting help. He needed a new challenge to help him forget the events of recent months, which had seen terrorism on his doorstep in Brighton and a former lover murdered.

Life was returning to normality and bringing with it a touch of boredom. He was superfluous to the smooth running of his bar, where Afina had everything under control, and he wasn't very good at sitting around doing nothing all day. Afina had suggested he should take up golf but the idea didn't appeal, especially given the recent April showers.

After a couple of minutes, Clara Buckingham swept into the room, followed by her husband. She was the epitome of elegance. Probably in her fifties, slim and attractive, she wore a simple black dress. It was the large, silver necklace which shouted out for attention. A stylish, short blond haircut and expertly applied makeup suggested she had certainly made an effort to impress. Or perhaps she always looked so manicured and perfect?

Her husband was dressed in a blue suit, white shirt and yellow tie. He must surely have dressed specifically for the meeting. Powell couldn't imagine anyone lounged around at home in such attire.

"Pleased to meet you Powell," Clara said in a cut-glass accent, as she approached. "Thank you so much for coming. Angela speaks very highly of you. In fact, she credits you with saving her life. Says she felt like committing suicide until you stepped in to help. She says you are resourceful, courageous and honest. She's quite a fan."

Powell stood up and returned the surprisingly firm handshake. "Good to meet you, Mrs Buckingham. Angela exaggerates."

"Please, call me Clara. And I hope she doesn't because you sound like exactly the person we need."

Charles Buckingham emerged from behind his wife. He was ruddy cheeked and bald. Despite the expensive cut of the suit, it only partially managed to hide the large belly. He was showing all the signs of someone who enjoyed too much fine dining.

"Charles Buckingham," he said, holding out his hand.

"Powell."

"I think you're just wasting your time but my wife is insistent we need your help." He threw his hands in the air and shrugged before sitting on the sofa.

Powell was a little taken aback by the less than effusive welcome but it was as he had surmised, Charles Buckingham was not entirely in favour of this meeting.

"Please take a seat," Clara suggested.

Powell sat back down in the armchair, leaving Clara to join her husband on the sofa. The maid entered and set down a tray containing freshly brewed coffee, milk, cups and saucers.

"We'll pour thanks, Rosa," Clara said and the maid left. "How do you take your coffee?" Clara asked, looking at Powell.

"I'll have mine quite milky, please," Powell replied. "No sugar."

Clara poured three cups and handed her husband black coffee without asking his preferences. Powell missed that closeness with a partner. The questions that didn't have to be asked and the familiarity of many years spent together.

It would soon be twenty five years since his wife was murdered. It was already two years since his daughter Bella was also murdered. How did the famous song go? *'Regrets, I've had a few; But then again, too few to mention.'* It wasn't true of his life. He had far too many regrets. He'd done it his way and in the case of his wife, she had been killed as a result.

Clara sat back in her chair. "I think I should explain our problem." After a brief pause to collect her thoughts she continued, "I believe our daughter Harriet is in danger." She again paused to allow the seriousness of what she had said to sink in. "Ten months ago she moved out and went to live in a commune near Haywards Heath." Clara found it difficult to say the word commune and made it sound like something unwelcome you might find on the sole of your shoe, after going for a walk.

"Full of bloody hippies," Charles added.

Clara gave her husband a cold stare before continuing. "She is a completely changed person. That man Scott seems to have mesmerised her."

"Who is Scott?" Powell asked.

"The man who runs the place," Clara explained. "He doesn't have a title or anything. At least, not that I know of, but he sets the rules and is in charge."

"And why do you believe Harriet is in danger?"

"She is out of her depth."

Aren't we all. Powell already had misgivings about the outcome of the meeting. He suspected Harriet was not so much in danger as acting against the wishes of her parents. "How old is Harriet?" he queried.

"Twenty," Clara answered. "She will be twenty one in four months."

"That's the bloody problem," Charles interjected. "She comes in to her inheritance at twenty one."

Powell thought it would be indiscrete to ask the sum but imagined it would be substantial. Instead he asked, "How was Harriet as a teenager? Has she always been a bit rebellious?"

"Not especially," Clara replied. "Since about seventeen she has used our house more as a hotel than a home but I think that's fairly normal for teenagers."

"So you don't think this is just a fad, which she will move on from when she becomes bored?"

"I'm very concerned," Clara replied. "She seems completely infatuated by this Scott fellow. She gave up her career to work on the commune's farm."

"It was hardly a career," Charles said sharply. "She was a receptionist in a film production company. Her main job was to look pretty."

"Have you met this Scott?" Powell asked.

"I have," Clara replied. "He's charming but must be at least fifteen years older than Harriet."

"Are they having a relationship?"

Again it was Clara who answered. "She came home for the weekend and I asked her that very question. She said they weren't in a relationship, it was just sex. She was trying to shock me but I didn't rise to the bait and asked her if she was at least taking precautions. She said most of the time it wasn't necessary because of his sexual preferences. She then asked me if I needed her to explain what she meant. I pointed out I hadn't found her under a bush and neither was it an immaculate conception so I understood perfectly well."

Powell was getting concerned his visit was going to be a complete waste of time. It seemed Harriet's mother simply objected to her daughter's lifestyle choices. "It does sound as if Harriet is happy. You said she was in danger. Frankly, I haven't heard anything to suggest she is in any danger."

"That same weekend, I went through her bag while she was walking the dog with Charles. I found a tin with something that looked like tobacco and some papers for rolling cigarettes. I'm not stupid. I know it was an illegal substance. She never did drugs until she met this Scott fellow."

Powell wondered if that was just wishful thinking. "Did you confront her about the drugs?"

"Of course I did and she just told me I was old fashioned, and screamed at me for going through her bag. Said there was nothing wrong with smoking an occasional joint. She thinks it will soon be legal in most countries."

"It is quite common amongst young people," Powell said gently.

"I'm not naïve and I'm not worried about her smoking a bit of weed. I tried it myself at university," Clara responded.

"Then what are you worried about?"

"When I went to parties at university, there were a number of students taking cocaine and other drugs. Most of my friends were wealthy and could afford to buy anything they wanted. One of the friends in my close circle died of an overdose. I'm worried Scott will introduce Hattie to hard drugs. I don't want her life ruined. She's already wasted the private schooling we provided."

"Do you think she may already be using other drugs?"

"I honestly don't know. She's argumentative and difficult but is that down to drugs or something else?"

"It might just be down to her being twenty and trying to find her own way in the world."

"Rubbish!" Charles joined in. "It's all down to this Scott person. I told her I didn't want her wasting her inheritance on drugs."

"What did she say?" Powell prompted.

"That it was her money and she would spend it however she wanted. We haven't seen or heard from her since."

"When was that?"

"About six weeks ago," Clara answered.

"Have you called her?"

"A hundred times but it always goes straight to voicemail."

"Are you worried something has happened to her?"

"We don't know what to think," Clara replied. "I contacted the police but they said there was nothing they could do. She's an adult and is free to join a commune and ignore us, if she wants. Obviously, I didn't mention my concerns about her taking drugs. I didn't want to get her in trouble."

"I'm sure she's perfectly safe," Charles added, with the first signs of sympathy for his wife. "That Scott fellow is having sex with Hattie, who is beautiful and half his age. She is also about to inherit a fortune. He must think he's won the bloody lottery. I don't think she could be any safer."

"Will you help us?" Clara asked desperately.

"I'm not sure what I can do," Powell replied. "I can't force Harriet to leave. In fact, any such attempted action is probably counterproductive. I assume you aren't proposing I kidnap her or anything quite so dramatic? Or illegal?"

"All I know is, we can't just leave her in that cult. Every day she spends there, I worry myself to death."

"Why do you now call it a cult and not a commune?" Powell asked. He wasn't entirely sure about the difference but the term cult did sound more threatening.

"She's being brainwashed," Clara answered emphatically. "Her personality has completely changed. We used to be very close. Now she's moody and argumentative. She never would have spoken to me like that in the past or not returned my calls."

Powell tried to choose his words carefully. "She's growing up. What you are describing is the sort of behaviour many parents face with their children. It's even possible, your antipathy to Scott and the whole idea of a commune has only driven her closer to him and his ideals." Powell was beginning to feel like a family guidance counsellor and it didn't seem appropriate.

"That's all very well," Charles butted in, obviously unimpressed with Powell's advice. "Hattie isn't just a rebellious youngster. She's an heiress."

"That may be true but she's still trying to find her way in the world."

"And what do we do about her inheritance?" Charles demanded.

"There is speculation on the internet that the commune is funded by donations from its members. I work in the City and asked a few questions. This Scott fellow has significant sums invested all over the place. He certainly didn't make that sort of money out of growing a few crops."

Powell understood why the Buckingham couple were concerned and especially the mother. He would have been devastated if Bella had ever done anything similar.

"Perhaps he has a private fortune or a rich benefactor?" Powell suggested.

"His only benefactors are the members of his commune," Charles replied, sharply. "Look up the definition of a commune. It says something like, a group of people living together and sharing possessions and responsibilities. I take possessions to include money."

"How much money does Harriet inherit on her birthday?"

"Twenty five million," Charles answered.

Powell was momentarily lost for words. It was an enormous amount of money, well beyond the sum he'd expected to hear. "Where exactly does this money come from?"

"Hattie's grandfather, left her the money in his will," Charles explained. "And I don't want her throwing it away. He worked hard all his life for that money."

"And her birthday is in four months?"

"August 16th to be precise," Clara answered. "We don't have much time."

"I'm still not sure what you expect from me."

"Check out this Scott," Charles answered. "I'm sure he's up to no good. We need to get some leverage on him so we can get him to stop manipulating our daughter."

It sounded like Charles wouldn't be averse to manipulating Scott, given the chance. He wanted Powell to dig up some dirt they could use as leverage, which sounded awfully like another name for blackmail.

"I'll do some preliminary enquiries and get back to you in a couple of weeks with what I discover," Powell suggested. "Of course, it may be I discover nothing. In the meantime, I'd try hard to build bridges with Harriet."

"Everyone calls her Hattie," Charles said. "Except Clara, who still insists on referring to her as Harriet despite having been asked not to do so a thousand times."

"She was christened Harriet and that's what I will call her," Clara said stubbornly.

"Do you have a recent picture of Harriet?" Powell asked. He'd been invited to the meeting by Clara and would observe her naming convention for her daughter.

Clara had obviously come prepared. She reached inside a pocket in her dress and produced a photo of an attractive young woman wearing a floral dress and a straw hat. Powell studied the subject of their conversation for the first time. Harriet was tall and slim, with very dark hair that fell to her shoulders. Her eyes were pools of darkness in an alabaster skin complexion and she was smiling broadly at the camera. She had a boyish or model like figure, depending on your personal choice of description. Whatever words you chose, there was no denying her beauty.

"It was taken about eighteen months ago at Henley, Clara explained. "In happier times, before she met Scott."

"She's very pretty," Powell acknowledged.

"She hasn't changed much in looks," Clara added.

"How did she meet Scott?" Powell asked.

"In a pub, I think she said. A couple of weeks later she moved into the commune."

"Was she experiencing any specific problems about that time?" Powell asked.

"No. The problems started once she joined that damned place," Charles answered, impatiently.

"There weren't any difficulties at home?"

"She wasn't running away from us, if that's what you mean,"

Charles retorted angrily. "Our only crime has been to give her everything she ever wanted. It's that Scott fellow you should be asking the questions. Not us."

"Sorry, I wasn't implying anything," Powell apologised. "I just wanted to understand better, Hattie's motives for joining the commune." He wouldn't be surprised if Harriett and her father had frequently argued. He was very opinionated.

"She's still very young and impressionable," Clara added. "She probably thinks she's in love. Whether that is truly with Scott or just the idea of being in love, I don't know. What I do know is that she needs our help."

"Does she have any strong religious beliefs?" Powell queried.

"Religion!" Clara laughed. "No. Harriet isn't religious."

"Okay. I'll be in touch soon," Powell said, standing to signal the meeting was finished. He felt he'd learned enough to get started.

"We can't let this Scott, get his hands on her money," Charles emphasised, climbing to his feet.

"It's not just about the money," Clara snapped.

"I'll see what I can find out," Powell promised.

He felt there was a definite undercurrent of hostility between husband and wife, which made him feel uncomfortable. He was also uncertain whether Charles Buckingham was more concerned for the money or his daughter's wellbeing. And why had he started the meeting so negatively? Perhaps it was just because his wife had organised the meeting. Powell thought Charles was a little pompous. Maybe he didn't take kindly to his wife making important decisions without fully consulting with him first. There was lots for Powell to consider on the way back to Brighton.

CHAPTER THREE

Powell spent a day on his computer, researching the commune and its leader but discovered nothing of great value. They had no web site and there was little information on the internet about the commune or Scott. The absence of anything negative was in fact a huge positive. He had feared he would read about a cult of devil worshippers.

There were no upset parents on any of the forums, complaining about or even mentioning the commune. Hattie's parents definitely seemed to be in a minority of one. Powell needed to find the names of other people living at the commune and check their backgrounds.

He found a people search web site, which allowed him to search on an address and back came a list of half a dozen people living at the commune address. It seemed most people living at the commune weren't bothered about adding themselves to the electoral register, which wasn't surprising. Hattie wasn't listed.

He decided against making a formal visit to the commune. He would probably learn nothing by a frontal assault. The commune was located in a large country house, called Tintagel, on the edge of the village of Lindfield, to the north-east of Haywards Heath, standing on the upper reaches of the River Ouse.

Powell smiled at the name. Tintagel was a castle in Cornwall associated with the legendary story of King Arthur. Powell decided the best place to start investigating would be the village pub. The regulars at any village pub tend to know the local gossip.

He decided to visit the pub at six when it would probably be relatively quiet and he might get a chance to chat to the people behind the bar. The drive from Brighton took just under thirty minutes and he was pleased to find the large pub car park was quite deserted when he arrived.

The pub was a traditional country pub, with old fashioned décor and furnishings, low ceilings and wooden beams. Powell walked up to the bar and studied the different beers for a minute. A pretty barmaid approached him and waited for his order. She seemed ridiculously young but then again so were some of the girls who worked in his bar. Another sure sign he was getting old.

"What can I get you?" the barmaid asked with a welcoming smile.

"You have a couple of beers I don't know."

"You can try one if you like?"

"Actually, I think I'll stick to what I know and have a pint of San Miguel," he said, giving his best smile. "This is a nice pub," he added, looking around.

"Thanks." She took a pint mug from under the shelf and started to pour his drink. "Is it your first time in here?"

"Yes, I've been looking at property in the area. I'm thinking of moving to somewhere around here."

"Where do you live now?"

"Brighton. I fancy moving somewhere a bit more in the country."

"I love Brighton," she said, putting his beer down on the counter. "That will be four pounds thirty, please."

Powell handed over a five pound note. "Does it get busy in here later?" he asked when she returned with his change.

"Not on a Tuesday night. There will be a few regulars but it gets busier at the weekend."

"I might try and chat to a few of the regulars. Find out what it's like to live around here."

"What would you like to know? I've lived around here for ever."

Powell sat himself on the bar stool. "Can I get you a drink?"

"Thanks. I'll have a glass of white wine but if you don't mind I'll save it for later. It's still a bit early."

Powell handed over another five pound note. There was even less change this time and he smiled at the recognition he might be some distance from Brighton but that wasn't reflected in the prices.

"I'm Powell by the way," he said, offering his hand.

"Lucy." She smiled and shook hands.

"So what's it like then, living around here?"

"Quiet. Not much happens. You have to go into Brighton for fun."

"Sounds perfect. I'm looking for somewhere quiet. Somewhere I can escape from the madness of everyday life. Someone was telling me today you even have a commune nearby."

"We do. Some of them come in here from time to time."

"I thought it was a spiritual retreat. Wouldn't think those types would frequent pubs."

"They're not religious or anything like that. Actually, they're a very friendly bunch. Never cause any trouble and like a few beers."

"Don't we all," Powell agreed, raising his glass and taking a drink. "I might even consider joining them now I know you can still have a drink."

Lucy smiled. "Rather you than me. One of the girls told me you can't have anything electronic at the house. Couldn't live without my phone."

"Do you work here fulltime, Lucy?"

"No. Just most evenings to make some money. I'm studying veterinary nursing at Plumpton college."

"So you like animals?"

"More than most humans," she laughed. "You know where you are with animals."

"We're not all bad; humans I mean."

"So what do you do?" Lucy asked.

"I own a bar in Brighton, well Hove to be specific. It pretty much runs itself, which is why I'm looking to move."

Another customer entered and Lucy excused herself to go take his order.

"What's your bar called?" Lucy asked, when she returned after a minute.

"Bellas."

"I know it!" Lucy exclaimed. "I've had lunch there. My friend Kate lives in Hove and took me there."

"I hope you enjoyed your visit." Powell awaited the verdict, as he always did, with a sense of trepidation.

"To be honest, I had a great time but my memory is a bit hazy. You serve a mean Mojito." Lucy smiled broadly before adding, "And I think the Caipirinhas were rather good as well."

"Sounds like it was a good lunch."

"It was great and continued well into the afternoon." She noticed another new customer enter the pub. "Excuse me a minute."

When Lucy returned, Powell requested, "If you see anyone enter from the commune, will you let me know. I'd like to find out more about the place."

"Will do. If you're staying round for a while, do you want to order some food?"

"That sounds a good idea." Now Powell had learned members of the commune drank in the pub, he was in no hurry to leave.

Lucy handed him a menu and he chose a large steak and chips. He decided to move to a table to eat his dinner and chose a corner table where he could watch everyone in the pub.

Over the next hour, a dozen people entered the pub and they all seemed to know each other, which suggested they were probably locals. Powell ordered a further pint but was drinking slowly as he was driving. It was eight when he noticed a young looking girl enter with a couple of men. Powell wasn't sure at first but once she removed her coat and hat, he was confident the girl was Hattie.

He thought one of the men could be Scott. He fitted the description given by Hattie's mother. The other man looked like someone who spent plenty of time in a gym, lifting weights. He could be a body builder. Powell revised his opinion as the man walked to the bar and ordered drinks. He was light on his feet, more like a boxer than a body builder.

Hattie and Scott had sat themselves at a table. After the boxer returned with the drinks, Hattie went up to the bar and spoke with Lucy. Powell watched as Hattie ordered some crisps but what really caught his eye was when Hattie passed over the money. He was quite sure she had passed Lucy more than just some money, though he couldn't be sure what had been in the palm of her hand.

Powell finished his beer and approached the bar. "One for the road, Lucy. Then I must be on my way."

"If you're still interested in finding out more about the commune, you're in luck. Those three are all members." Lucy nodded in the direction of Hattie's table.

"Thanks. I'll go have a word." Powell picked up his new beer and headed for the table.

"Lucy at the bar said you were the right people to have a word with about the commune," Powell said, as he reached the table.

Scott looked up and replied, "What was it you wanted to know?"

"Well I was wondering if it was somewhere you could go if you were looking to get away for a while? I mean really escape from the material world, like a retreat."

"I'm Scott. Pull up a chair and I can answer your questions."

"My name's Powell. I'm not intruding am I?"

"We were just chilling. This is Hattie and Tommy."

Powell shook each hand and sat in the spare chair. "It's good to meet you all."

"So Powell, if you don't mind my asking, what is it that makes you interested in escaping from the world?" Scott asked.

Powell appeared as if he was struggling with difficult memories, which in truth he was, before answering. "My daughter died about two years ago. She was murdered and I'm on my own now. My wife was also murdered when Bella was just a small child. Bella was my daughter. That was about twenty years ago. Then there were the recent terrorist attacks in Brighton, which killed one of my friends. I just need to get away somewhere and clear my head. Spend some time deciding what I want to do with the rest of my life."

"I'm sorry to hear about your family," Scott said. "I'm sure you understand we are very careful who we allow to join our group. We have to be certain anyone new will fit in. We are a very close knit group."

"I understand. How many of you are there?"

"Twenty four. We have eight men and sixteen women. To be honest a couple more men wouldn't go amiss."

"I second that," Hattie said with a big smile.

"What do you do for a living?" Scott asked. "Are you going to be able to take time away from work?"

"I own a bar in Brighton, which runs by itself. Or at least I have a very good manager. Time isn't an issue."

"Okay so how about you come and spend a day with us and see what you think," Scott suggested. "We all share the work and it isn't suitable for everyone."

Powell smiled broadly. "I've never been afraid of hard work. When would be suitable for me to pay a visit?"

"How about Thursday?" Scott asked.

"Fine with me."

"You can spend the day with Hattie. She can show you around and introduce you to a few of the others. Then we can have a chat at the end of the day. See whether you are still interested."

"What time should I come?"

"Come about ten," Hattie answered. "You can join us in our morning prayers for a couple of hours."

"Don't worry," Scott quickly interjected. "Hattie is just teasing. Although I consider myself spiritual, we are certainly not a religious group in the accepted sense and don't spend time on our knees praying. If that is what you are looking for then you should try to join a monastery."

"I've rather given up on religion," Powell explained. "I have no problem with people having faith but it seems to me religion or at least the institutions of each religion, have been responsible for more harm than good."

"I think we will get on just fine," Scott said.

"I must be going," Powell said rising. "I need to get back to Brighton. I'll see you all on Thursday. Enjoy the rest of your evening."

Powell returned to the bar, left his half-finished beer on the counter and thanked Lucy for her help.

As Powell walked to his car, he was very satisfied with his evening's work. He had found Scott to be very friendly. Clara Buckingham had called him a charmer. Powell sensed she was probably right in her view.

Powell did wonder if it was a coincidence, once he mentioned he owned a bar, Scott was very quick to invite him to visit the commune. But he wouldn't jump to conclusions. He didn't want to be influenced by the negative views of Charles Buckingham.

Seeing Hattie for the first time, had been an interesting experience. He was fairly sure he had seen her pass something to Lucy. The fact she hadn't wanted anyone else in the pub to see what she was doing, did suggest it could be drugs. Even if it was, it might only be a joint and that wold be no reason for her parents to panic. Despite Clara's concerns, most young people who enjoyed a joint, didn't automatically move on to harder drugs.

Tommy was curious. He seemed out of place in the company of the others. He hadn't said a word and still reminded Powell of a boxer or a bouncer. Perhaps he was just the strong, silent type. Powell decided he would have to keep an eye on Tommy.

CHAPTER FOUR

Powell had given his name to a gruff sounding male at the other end of the entry system and explained he was meeting with Hattie. There was no immediate response but after a pause, he was instructed to drive up to the main house. He had obviously been checking Powell was expected.

The double gates swung open and Powell glimpsed the inside of the estate for the first time. He had observed the cameras at the gate and the high, thick walls. The security measures certainly protected the privacy of those inside. Was the intention to keep people away or make it difficult for those living at the house to leave?

The driveway leading to the house wound its way through woodland and then emerged on to a vast lawn. There were large numbers of daffodils and tulips in circular flower beds. The sun was shining and Spring was definitely in the air.

Powell could see Hattie waiting for him on the steps of the grand house. It was very imposing and must once have belonged to someone important and very wealthy. Hattie was dressed very casually in jeans and a sweater. Her hair was tied back in a ponytail. Nothing about the way she looked, suggested she was wealthy.

"You actually came!" Hattie exclaimed as Powell stepped out of the car.

"I said I would."

"But you had a few beers and I thought you might wake up and change your mind."

"I'm excited to be here," Powell smiled. "Even more so now I've seen this place. It's a mansion not a house."

Hattie kissed him on each cheek in greeting. "It's Georgian, built in seventeen ninety and we have seventy seven acres of grounds but that's the extent of my knowledge."

"Well it's certainly impressive."

"I'll give you a quick tour of the house and then we can grab a coffee and I can answer more of your questions," she suggested.

"Are there any rules I need to know about while I'm here?" Powell asked.

"Rules? No, we lead a very liberal lifestyle. Most of us aren't very keen on rules. We do have a kind of charter. We agree to show love, respect and tolerance to each other. Ask anyone anything you want."

Powell was learning to like Hattie. She had an infectious enthusiasm. He wondered how her parents would react if he reported back something they didn't want to hear?

Hattie led the way through various rooms on the ground floor, including a very impressive library, which Powell perused for a few minutes.

"I'm a big reader," he explained. "Who do all the books belong to?"

"They came with the house. Feel free to help yourself."

"Thanks. This collection would keep me busy for a very long time."

"I'm not much of a reader myself," Hattie admitted. "I prefer the outdoors."

"I like the outdoors as well. I enjoy camping in remote places and long walks. But when you get back to your tent for the evening, then I enjoy a good book."

"That's when I like to open a bottle of something and chill out with whoever I'm with. Reading is such a lonely hobby. I prefer to interact with people."

"Hey, I like to interact with people," Powell retorted. I'm honestly not old and boring just because I like to read."

"I never said you were. I just think there's better things to do in a tent late at night, than read a book," Hattie hinted. She smiled broadly and he wondered for the first time whether perhaps it was Hattie who had seduced Scott and not the other way around.

Powell smiled in return. "As I said, I'm not old and boring," he stressed. "It's just I tend to go camping by myself so interaction with others is a bit limited come the evening."

"Now I understand," Hattie nodded. "And interaction with yourself is definitely not as much fun as with other people."

Powell understood her innuendo and smiled. "You're trouble," he said succinctly.

"Only in a fun way."

"Let's change the subject," Powell proposed. He wondered if he was blushing. "Who owns this house?"

"Scott. I think he bought the place at auction after the previous owner died."

Powell had researched the ownership on the internet and found the property was owned by a company, which described its business as property management. Scott wasn't listed as a director of the company so Powell wondered if Hattie was just assuming Scott was the owner.

They carried on with their tour of the house. There was a huge living room and a games room with a table tennis table.

"Do you play?" Hattie asked.

"I used to as a kid."

"We have regular competitions. They get quite competitive. Sometimes we play for interesting prizes."

"What sort of prizes?"

"You will have to enter one of the tournaments to find out."

Powell's imagination was working overtime conjuring up loads of possible prizes. He didn't think Hattie was referring to anything as mundane as medals.

Next they visited the oak panelled dining room and what was described as the quiet living room.

"This is a room for reading and reflection," Hattie whispered, even though it was empty. Then she added with a grin, "It doesn't get used very much."

"Sounds perfect. I'll have a room all to myself. You're lucky to be living in such an amazing house."

"You must come and join us," Hattie answered with another

beaming smile. "You'd fit in well. You have a good sense of humour."

"I like what I've seen so far," Powell admitted.

Hattie led the way to the kitchen where two women were preparing food for lunch and dinner.

"I can cook a bit," Powell announced.

"Really?" Hattie questioned doubtfully. "None of the other men are any use in the kitchen."

"My bar serves good food," he answered by way of explanation. "I've spent plenty of time in the kitchen."

On the second floor, Powell was shown the sleeping arrangements. There were about a dozen bedrooms. Some had multiple beds in the room.

Standing inside one of the larger rooms, which had the biggest double bed he'd ever seen, he asked, "How is it decided who sleeps where?"

"You sleep where you want," she answered. Then added, "And with whom you want."

"I was going to ask about that. Are the men in relationships with the women?"

"Scott doesn't believe in fixed relationships. He thinks it is more harmonious if we simply love who we want, when we want."

Powell could see Hattie was appraising him, waiting to see his reaction.

"And if like me, you aren't looking for any form of harmonious relationship?"

"You're not gay are you?"

"Would it matter if I was?"

"Of course not. I was just interested."

"Well I'm not gay."

"The girls will be pleased to hear that."

"But neither am I looking for any form of relationship."

"Let's get some coffee," Hattie suggested. "You've seen most of the house."

Back in the kitchen, Hattie made some filter coffee and they then returned to the living room.

"Where is everyone?" Powell asked when they were seated.

"Working. Scott will be in his office. The rest are working outside. It's Scott's goal for us to become completely self-sufficient. We grow all our own fruit and vegetables. We also have a couple of cows, some hens and chickens. And of course, there's good fishing in the lake."

"How do the finances work? I assume we don't all get to stay here for free."

"Everybody contributes according to their means. Those who have more, give more. I'm sure Scott will discuss the details with you later."

"Sounds very fair." The thought crossed Powell's mind that Charles Buckingham might be right to be worried about Hattie's inheritance.

"Scott is a great believer in fairness. I'm sure you will love it here. It's a great place to contemplate what's important in life."

"Sounds like you've worked out what's important to you."

"Well let's say I know what isn't important."

"Are we allowed to bring laptops and phones?" Powell asked.

"I'm sorry, most of us have come here to get away from the material and electronic world so we have agreed not to bring electronic gadgets into the house. Scott has a computer and a phone in his office, which are available for emergencies. Is that a problem?"

"Not for me," Powell confirmed. "I'm not one of those people who walk around staring at a phone all day. I think it's an age thing. When I was young, mobile phones didn't even exist."

It explained why Hattie's phone always went straight to voicemail. She was obviously infatuated with Scott and the way of life he offered but she was also a bright girl and Powell couldn't imagine her handing over all her millions to Scott, the minute she was twenty one.

"So what is the worst thing about living here?" Powell asked.

Hattie seemed taken aback by the question. After a few seconds she answered, "I suppose it's a bit like living with a very large family. We see a lot of each other and every so often you fall out over something."

"Don't you miss having your own room and privacy?"

"I go for a walk when I want to be by myself. It's easy to lose yourself in the grounds."

"How do you come to be here?" Powell asked.

"A friend of a friend told me about the place and I was looking to get away from a very claustrophobic home environment. My parents haven't really adjusted to the idea that I've grown up. I came down for a weekend and I've been living here ever since."

"What do your family think about you being here?"

"They don't understand me. My father is too wrapped up in making money and my mother worries I've joined a cult of religious nuts. As I said, they treat me like I'm still a child."

"All parents worry about their children. Remember they brought you in to the world and may not be around for ever so try not to fallout."

"I do love them but they make everything so difficult. I care about the planet much more than about making money. I will choose who I love and it won't be determined by their social status." Hattie realised she had raised her voice and become animated. "Sorry," she apologised with a smile. "Scott says I should put things right with my parents. I've been ignoring them because they made me so mad. Scott says I should accept my parents as they are. He doesn't believe they will ever change. They are a product of their upbringing and they belong to a different generation."

"I agree with Scott." Powell was surprised and pleased to hear Scott was encouraging Hattie to get back in touch with her parents. He wasn't trying to isolate her from them, which he would be doing if he had any sinister intentions.

"Are you similarly old fashioned?" Hattie asked. "After all, you are quite old yourself."

Powell smiled. He recognised he was being teased. "Only in years. I'm still waiting to grow up," he quipped.

Hattie smiled. "Scott was right. You should fit in well. You have a sense of humour."

"I hope so. Speaking of Scott, how long has he been running the commune?"

"You can ask him later. I think it's about time I showed you around the grounds."

CHAPTER FIVE

Powell returned to Brighton, having agreed with Scott, he would return for a one month trial. Scott explained everyone initially moved in on a trial basis and nearly everyone had extended their stay once the trial period was finished.

Powell told Afina he would be gone a maximum of a month and despite her obvious curiosity, he told her little about where he was going. He needed some time alone to recharge his batteries. The recent terrorist attacks, which had resulted in the death of Lara, had left him in need of a break.

In an emergency, he could be contacted through the number he provided, which was the phone in Scott's office. But it was only to be used for absolute emergencies, not to discuss changes in the menu.

In truth, he expected to be away far less time than a month because he believed he was on a wild goose chase. Hattie seemed both physically safe and compos mentis. Whatever her feelings for Scott, she still seemed perfectly capable of making her own rational decisions. For his part, Scott didn't seem over controlling and ran a relaxed commune. Either that or he had put on a good act for Powell, in order to get him to return.

Powell didn't believe Hattie would hand over all her millions to Scott or that he would exert any undue influence on her to do so. She might contribute some amount but even as much as a million dollars would only make a relatively small dent in her fortune. It might give Charles Buckingham a heart attack but he wasn't exactly short of a penny or two.

However, Powell had learned nothing in life was certain so he would spend a bit longer with the commune rather than just provide Hattie's parents with his brief, initial thoughts. He wasn't interested in extending his assignment for financial reward but he didn't want to be accused of making hasty decisions. Clara Buckingham deserved his best efforts even if he wouldn't cross the road to help her husband .

Powell doubted he would be able to influence Hattie with regard to how she spent her money and he had no intention of trying to do so. He hoped he would be able to put Hattie's parents' minds at rest about their daughter's safety but he was not going to get in the middle of a family war about how she spent her inheritance or lived her life.

The day after his first visit to Tintagel, he returned with a suitcase of clothes and was again greeted by Hattie. She asked him to confirm he hadn't brought a phone or any form of electronic devices before showing him to a bed in a room with three single beds.

"Scott suggested I put you in here to start with," Hattie explained with a mischievous smile.

"Are the other two beds occupied?"

"Not usually."

"What do you mean by putting me here to start with?"

"I think you will be getting some serious interest from one or two of the girls."

"Perhaps you could do me a favour and just mention to everyone that I'm really not looking for any female attention. In the very unlikely event there is some interest, I don't want to hurt anyone's feelings."

"As you wish," Hattie replied doubtfully. "But I'm not sure it will make any difference. Some of the girls will just see it as a challenge to get you to sleep with them. Others are simply desperate for the company of a new man."

"If you don't mind my saying, you are making me wonder what sort of a place I've joined," Powell said lightly with a grin.

"We work hard and play hard. Scott advocates a very open culture. What can be more natural than the physical expression of our feelings?"

Powell could tell he was being teased a little but also perhaps tested.

"Call me old fashioned but I like to get to know someone before entering into a physical relationship. I find it makes for better sex."

"It's probably a generational thing. You are as old as my parents and I don't think they even have sex."

"I wouldn't be too sure about that. Sex is not just the preserve of the young and beautiful."

"So you do like sex?"

"You could teach some of the Newsnight team interrogation, I mean interview techniques."

"Sorry, I am very direct."

"That's okay. I'm not easily offended." Not for the first time around Hattie, Powell decided to change the subject. "Where did you decide to put me to work?"

"You said you were good at most DIY skills so Scott thought you could work on the long list of things that need fixing around the house. We have leaking pipes, electrics not working and a host of other jobs."

"Sounds right up my street. Point me in the right direction."

"Dave has been trying to do these jobs for us but the list gets longer quicker than he can fix things. He's working in one of the bathrooms so I'll take you to him and then I'll catch up with you later."

For Powell, the rest of the day passed quickly. Dave turned out to be an uncomplicated Welshman, who needed very little encouragement to get him singing. Almost anything Powell said would trigger a song. Fortunately, he had an excellent voice and Powell enjoyed his company. It was good for the spirit, to spend a day fixing things.

Dinner was at seven and everyone was seated at the long dining table. Powell sat himself next to Hattie and was quickly surrounded by some of the other women. As the new man, he found himself subjected to a barrage of questions, which in the main he was able to answer honestly. His basic cover story was that the loss of his daughter, followed by the death of his friend at the hands of terrorists, had left him questioning the meaning of life and in need of a quiet sanctuary.

He gently probed why others were at the commune and most people seemed to be either running away from pain or searching for a more spiritual way of life. There were repeated comments about how the world had become too materialistic and mankind was destroying the planet. Powell kept his views to himself but he couldn't see how hiding away in a commune was helping solve the world's problems.

Powell noticed Scott sat at one end of the table, rather like the Lord of the manor. Tommy from the pub sat on one side of Scott and another man, he learned was called Roger, on the other side. Powell hadn't seen either man during the previous day's tour of the house and gardens or today. Where had they been hiding away and what exactly did they do for Scott?

They didn't seem to fit in like the other members of the commune. Powell very much doubted whether they were at the commune for spiritual reasons. They stuck out like a sore thumb. Perhaps they were some form of security, which invited the question, why did Scott feel he needed security? Who or what were they protecting Scott from?

He would ask Hattie about them but he needed to be careful. Over lunch, he had gained the impression, Hattie was reluctant to answer any questions about Scott. Powell didn't want to seem too inquisitive and make Hattie suspicious.

After a meal of pasta with a vegetable sauce made from fresh ingredients grown in the garden, a couple of the women invited him to join them for a cigarette.

"Thanks but I don't smoke," Powell declined with a smile.

"This isn't tobacco we're smoking," an attractive woman in her thirties revealed. Powell was struggling to remember many people's names.

"I don't smoke *anything*," Powell emphasised. "I'm a bit of a fitness fanatic and run marathons." He had run the Brighton marathon one time but his fitness was really derived from his kickboxing training. That wasn't something he felt he needed to share with his new friends.

"You look pretty fit," the woman said, making no attempt to disguise the fact she was flirting. "I might have to take up running." She walked away before he could answer.

"Looks like you've sparked Carol's interest," Hattie laughed. "I did warn you."

"You did indeed."

"I didn't know you were a runner," Hattie continued. "A group of us go running every morning around the grounds. If you want to join us, be at the front of the house at seven. That's as long as you realise we aren't Olympic athletes."

"I'll probably give it a miss, thanks. I prefer to run by myself. That way I can set my own pace. I tend to awake about six and run for an hour."

"Suit yourself. Do you fancy a game of table tennis?"

"I haven't played in years but sounds a good idea." He remembered Hattie's comment about playing for interesting prizes. "I assume we are just playing for fun not prizes?"

"Don't look so scared. It's just for fun… This time!"

As they walked to the games room, Powell noticed Scott and his two shadows leaving the house. Perhaps they were off to the pub.

Powell's table tennis skills were proven to be inadequate to compete with the others and it was a good job there were no prizes at stake. He decided to see what was happening in the living room.

He spotted Carol and another female chatting and drinking from mugs. They both smiled in his direction when he entered the room. As he wanted to find out more about life in the house, he decided to join them.

"How are you settling in?" Carol asked.

"So far, so good," he replied. "But my table tennis skills aren't up to scratch."

"How about your other skills?" Carol asked with a cheeky smile.

Powell simply smiled in response.

"We haven't met," he said, turning to the second woman and

holding out his hand.

"Kirsty," she replied, taking his hand. "Good to meet you." She was a red head with pale skin and a face full of freckles. She was about thirty years of age and spoke with a Yorkshire accent.

"So how long have you two lived here?"

"We both joined about eighteen months ago," Kirsty answered.

"So I guess you enjoy it here?"

"We do," Carol answered. "Here you can be yourself. You don't have to pretend to be something you're not."

"Why are you here?" Kirsty asked.

"I suppose I'm running away."

"From what?" Carol asked.

Powell realised how what he'd said might be interpreted wrongly. "I'm not a murderer or anything," he laughed. "I just needed to get away from everything. I needed time to think about life."

"I think you'll like it here," Kirsty said with conviction. "And if you discover the meaning of life be sure to let me in on the secret."

"I will," Powell promised.

"Would you like to celebrate your arrival by partying with us?" Carol asked.

"I fear I'm going to seem very boring but I need an early night."

"That's exactly what I was suggesting," Carol smiled.

"Maybe another time," Powell suggested.

"Perhaps he has already made arrangements for tonight," Kirsty suggested.

"What do you mean?" Powell enquired.

"You seemed to be getting on very well with Hattie," Kirsty replied.

"I would be careful with Hattie," Carol cautioned. "She and Scott are very close."

"I thought Scott believed in the free expression of our physical emotions."

"That's what he says but he treats Hattie special," Carol answered.

Powell sensed a hint of jealousy. Perhaps life in the house wasn't quite as harmonious as he'd been led to believe. "Look, I'm just not in the mood to party."

"Would you like something to put you in the mood?" Carol persisted.

"What do you have?" Powell asked out of curiosity.

"We have most things. I like a joint but there's coke if that's your poison and a variety of pills. The only pills we don't have are the blue ones but think of us as the equivalent."

"Sorry," Kirsty quickly interjected. "I love Carol but she has a bit of a one track mind sometimes."

"No need to apologise. I'm flattered by the idea two such gorgeous women would want to party with me. But one of the reasons I'm here is a recent lover of mine was killed by terrorists. So you see, I really don't feel like any form of partying."

"That's awful," Carol said. "I'm so sorry."

"But I hope we can still be friends," Powell stated.

"Of course," both women answered in unison.

"We are all friends here," Carol added glibly.

"Good. I'll see you both tomorrow. I'm off to bed."

CHAPTER SIX

Scott arrived at the meeting wondering what was so urgent that it couldn't wait until the next day. He didn't enjoy having his evening plans interrupted at short notice. The headlights on the approaching car signalled its arrival long before it came to a halt. The country lane didn't see much traffic, which was why it made a good spot to meet. It was the only other car Scott had seen in the ten minutes he'd been parked, waiting for them to arrive.

The car parked directly in front of Scott's Land Rover, leaving the other side of the road free for any passing traffic. As was the routine, Scott stepped out of his car and walked to the Renault. He didn't want his muscle knowing all the details of his business. A view he knew was shared by the occupants of the Renault.

Scott sat in the back seat. The front seats were both occupied.

"So what is so important you couldn't tell me over the phone?" Scott asked without preamble.

The man in the front passenger seat turned around to face Scott. He was in his mid-thirties and had a round face. He shaved his head to hide the fact he was going bald but had a large, bushy moustache. "Someone's been asking questions about your place," he answered. "Someone with clout."

"Who?"

"Don't know specifically but it's probably someone in the security services."

"Are you sure?"

"That it was the security services? No, I'm not bloody sure but my boss hinted as much."

"Why would the security services be interested in us?"

"I was hoping you could tell me."

"I've no idea. What did you tell them, Doug?"

"I wrote a brief report, which in summary said you weren't on our radar. But why the bloody hell are MI5 asking about you in the first place?"

"I don't know but it could be Hattie's father. He's loaded and probably has friends in high places."

"You don't seem very worried," Doug said.

"I don't think there's any reason to panic. They wouldn't be asking you such questions if, even for a second, they suspected our relationship so you're obviously in the clear."

"I hadn't thought of it like that. Unless it's a trap and they were seeing how I would respond."

"In which case there's probably a bunch of spooks about to jump out from the trees," Scott warned.

Doug immediately glanced to the trees on the side of the road.

"Don't get too paranoid," Scott continued. "MI5 are interested in catching terrorists so we definitely fall outside their normal remit. If someone was after you, it wouldn't be MI5. Therefore, I think it's more likely to be an unofficial enquiry. Someone doing a favour for a friend."

"I hope you're right."

"I'll speak to Hattie and get her back in touch with her family. They haven't heard from her for a long while, which might explain them wanting to check up on us. She can find out if they are responsible for raising your blood pressure."

Scott had told Hattie she shouldn't shun her family. They would be worried and it might lead to trouble. The last thing he wanted was her parents making his life difficult.

"Perhaps we should lay low for a while," Doug suggested.

"I have made promises," Scott replied. "If I stop supplying then someone else will take my customers. I can't allow that to happen."

"Okay but we need to tread carefully."

"We should always tread carefully," Scott emphasised. "Our business arrangement has been highly profitable for both of us. In fact, demand is so high, I would like to double the size of our next order."

Doug raised his eyebrows in surprise. "That's a big increase."

"Is it a problem for you?"

"No, it's not a problem," Doug quickly replied. "I will just need a little more time to source the extra supply."

"Is a week long enough?"

"A week is fine."

"Good. Now I want to get back to the house. Much as I enjoy your company, I had a different sort of evening planned."

"You lucky bugger," Doug said, obviously jealous. "You get all the perks."

Scott returned to his car in thoughtful mood. He had appeared more relaxed by Doug's revelations than was the reality. He didn't like the idea of anyone prying into his business.

He hoped he was right in his assertion it was Hattie's father checking them out. He was a known problem, which Scott could handle. Anyone else poking around might signal a risk to his plans. He would make a call in the morning and determine whether he had cause to be concerned.

CHAPTER SEVEN

Powell was up at six and dressed quietly in his running gear so as not to wake anyone else in the house. He'd slept well and not been disturbed by any attractive women trying to sneak into his bed in the middle of the night. He was sure Hattie had been wildly exaggerating the likelihood of such an event. He'd been taken in by the whole preposterous idea, actually believing it was a possibility. It brought a smile to his face.

There were no signs of life as he went downstairs and out through the front door. He breathed deeply and did a few stretching exercises before heading off at a fast pace. Even though he had only been living in Tintagel a short time, he found it claustrophobic and was pleased to be outdoors.

It was a good morning for running. A bright sunny day lay ahead with little prospect of any April showers. The cool early morning weather was perfect for running.

Powell thought about what he'd so far discovered as he ran. He was fast becoming aware that life at Tintagel followed few normal conventions. The relaxed attitude to sex was matched by a similarly liberal approach to drugs. While Hattie's parents might not approve of such behaviour, Powell wasn't sure there was anything sinister about Scott or the commune.

Powell realised he didn't want to spend weeks living at the house so he was going to have to move things along. Scott's office was the only room in the house which was locked and might hide secrets. He would have to take a look inside once everyone went to bed.

The day passed much like the previous one. He spent time with Dave, fixing various problems around the house. He was slowly getting to know more people and found everyone to be welcoming and friendly.

"Can you drive me to the supermarket?" Hattie asked, late in the afternoon. "I could do with some help with the heavy items."

"Of course," Powell answered, pleased to have the opportunity to spend time just with Hattie.

It took twenty minutes to reach the out of town supermarket. Powell had driven the shared Land Rover, which belonged to the commune in general rather than anyone in particular and with its huge boot was perfect for a large shopping expedition. He was surprised by how few of the residents had their own car at the house.

With two large trolleys filled to the brim, he realised why Hattie had asked for his help. They pushed the trolleys towards the car and Powell unlocked the boot.

He noticed the two young men approach but continued putting the groceries in the back of the Land Rover.

"Hello Hattie," one of the men said, as they came close.

Powell noticed there was no welcoming smile on Hattie's face.

"What do you want, Steve?" she asked, obviously annoyed by their presence.

"Pete and I thought you could help us out. We really need something."

Powell looked closer at the two young men. They both looked scruffy and their hair was unkempt. Their eyes were darting from side to side. Powell could identify the signs of drug use.

"You still owe me from the last time," Hattie answered, in a sharp tone. "Have you got my money?"

"Don't be like that," Steve said. "We just want a small hit. You'll get your money."

"I'm not your fairy godmother and I don't run a charity."

Powell had stopped loading the bags and was now watching the two men closely.

"You heard the lady," Powell said pleasantly. "Come back when you have some money."

Steve completely ignored Powell's comment. He took a couple of steps nearer to Hattie and withdrew a long knife with a serrated edge from his belt.

"Give me something now and I won't cut you, bitch," Steve threatened.

"Do it," Pete encouraged. "Cut the bitch. She deserves it."

Powell acted quickly. He took two paces towards Steve and as he started to turn, Powell grabbed the wrist holding the knife and twisted it up behind his back, causing Steve to drop the knife. Powell thrust Steve up against the side of the Land Rover.

"You shouldn't play with knifes," Powell warned. "Someone might get hurt."

Driven by desperation, Pete threw himself at Powell without warning. Powell turned Steve back to face his friend and pushed him in Pete's direction, causing them both to fall to the ground. They were both skinny and offered no real threat so Powell did nothing further.

"Get in the car, Hattie," he instructed.

Steve was first back on his feet. "I'll fucking make you pay for that," he threatened.

"Go home before you get hurt," Powell suggested. "Otherwise, you'll be leaving here in the back of an ambulance."

Pete had joined Steve on his feet. "Perhaps we should go," Pete said.

"Not before Hattie gives us what we want," Steve answered. He was obviously the more desperate of the two.

Steve took a couple of steps forward while his friend hung back. Powell advanced and in a blur of movement, struck a punch to Steve's midriff, leaving him bent double and in agony.

Powell gave Pete a questioning look, which was met with him taking a couple of steps backwards and nodding vigorously. He was definitely more intelligent than his friend.

Without further ado, Powell joined Hattie in the car and accelerated away. He waited for Hattie to speak.

"Thanks for your help," Hattie said after a minute. "I don't know what they might have done if you hadn't been there."

"Well I was there. Who were they?"

"Local crackheads. How did you manage to take that knife off him so easily?"

"As you said, they were just crackheads. I've done a bit of kickboxing in the past."

"You're full of surprises, Powell."

"You better not go shopping alone in the near future."

"I like your style, Powell. You haven't bothered suggesting we report them to the police. That's cool. You know I've sold them drugs and would get in trouble. Thanks."

"What you do or don't sell is none of my business."

"I like you, Powell. If you feel like some company tonight, be sure to let me know." She smiled very seductively and Powell's heart missed a beat but he wouldn't be taking her up on her offer.

Back at Tintagel, Hattie helped unload the shopping and then went to find Scott. He listened to Hattie retell the events at the supermarket.

"I'll speak to Doug and have him sort them out," he said, when she'd finished. "I'm sorry you had to experience that."

"It would have been very scary if Powell hadn't been with me."

"Powell seems very capable in many ways. I'm hearing good things about his work."

"I like him. I hope he stays."

"I'll thank him personally later. Now I have a few things to do before dinner, if you don't mind?"

Hattie took the hint and left Scott to his work. She felt like a drink and headed to the kitchen as it was almost time for lunch, which meant the wine would be available for the next hour. She poured a large glass of white wine and not wanting company, headed to the reading room.

"Didn't think you used this room," Powell said as Hattie entered.

"I wasn't feeling hungry but I did need a drink," Hattie explained, holding up her glass before sitting in an armchair.

"Are you okay?"

"I'm fine. Especially now I have a drink."

"You might be experiencing some of the after effects of shock."

Hattie took a large drink of wine. "I'm feeling better already."

"I'll leave," Powell suggested. "If you want some time alone."

"Don't go. I didn't want to answer endless questions from everyone else but you're okay."

"Thanks. Let's talk about something else. Tell me about Hattie. What was life like growing up?"

"I can't complain. I had everything I wanted."

"You didn't say that with conviction," Powell challenged.

"It's strange but I never remember being cuddled or kissed as a child. When I have children, I intend to kiss them and let them know I love them, every day."

"You mean your parents didn't easily show affection?"

"No. They bought me things but I was an only child and I often felt very alone."

"What are your parents like?" Powell asked.

"My mum is okay but she's always worried what someone else will think of her. She lives her life constrained by social rules."

"And your dad?"

"My stepdad never really wanted me around. I was an inconvenience."

Powell was shocked to discover Charles wasn't Hattie's real father. "But I've heard you refer to him as your father in the past."

"Mum encouraged me to call him Dad when I was growing up. It's only as I was older, I started referring to him sometimes as my stepfather. It irritated him."

What happened to your real dad?"

"He was killed in a speedboat accident when I was just two years old. I never knew him."

"I'm sorry."

"My mother thinks I'm searching for a father figure in Scott. She may be right but I just find him hot as hell!" Hattie laughed.

Powell was realising Hattie's life had been more complicated than he first imagined. "Well us men are like fine wine. We get better with age."

Scott was thinking about Powell and how his arrival had coincided with Doug reporting that someone, possibly MI5, was asking questions. Scott had heard the story about Powell's girlfriend being killed by terrorists. Where there were terrorists, there would be MI5 not far behind.

Perhaps Powell was actually the target of MI5's interest. Maybe they were keeping tabs on him and his presence at Tintagel had led to the questions. It might all be routine. It was food for thought. Scott didn't want MI5 accidentally stumbling across his business, while they were keeping an eye on Powell.

He needed to remain calm and not jump to conclusions. It could all be a coincidence and it was probably still Hattie's parents poking around but he would have Doug check out Powell. This wasn't the right time to have someone meddling in his affairs.

CHAPTER EIGHT

Doug knew where Steve and Pete lived. He organised a raid on their property for early in the morning. A time when he knew they would be sleeping off the previous night's excesses. He doubted they ever crawled out of their beds before midday.

A Sergeant broke down the front door with a battering ram and officers poured into the filthy flat, they called home. Doug followed them into the lounge just as the two men were being rousted from their beds. Looking dishevelled, the two suspects were dragged into the living room, noisily complaining about the intrusion.

"This is a violation of our human rights," Pete complained.

Doug tried not to laugh. Where the hell had Pete learned that phrase? Nowadays, it seemed every petty crook and waster was going on about their human rights. "We have a warrant to search these premises," he explained. "It's all perfectly legal."

"Don't you lot make a mess," Steve demanded.

Doug had no idea how they would ever notice the difference to the current state of the place. Doug had seen tidier squats.

He went to the kitchen, took the small white bag of powder from his pocket and placed it in a jar on the side, which contained a few tea bags. He made a bad job of covering the powder with the tea bags and quickly returned to the lounge.

The two men were sitting on the sofa, fidgeting uncomfortably like they needed a fix.

"I'm not staying here," Pete said and started to rise from the sofa.

One of the officers shoved him back down, none too gently.

"You can't touch me," Pete complained. "It's against my human rights."

"I'm Inspector Williams," Doug interrupted. "As has already been explained to you, we have a warrant to search this property. Please sit quietly while we do our job. Otherwise, I will have you put in handcuffs and charged with assault."

"I haven't assaulted anyone!" Pete exclaimed.

"Then sit there and don't move," Doug ordered.

Pete did as he was told. He suddenly grinned and said, "You won't find anything. We're what you might call short at the moment."

Short of a few brain cells, Doug thought.

The Sergeant instructed three officers where to start searching. One was despatched to the bedroom, one remained in the living room and the third went to the kitchen.

The suspects sat in silence until a shout from the kitchen alerted Doug and the Sergeant that something had been found.

Doug went to the kitchen and acted as a witness to the discovery of the cocaine stash, which had been in his pocket only ten minutes earlier.

Returning to the lounge, Doug left the Sergeant to read the suspects their rights.

"That isn't ours," Pete screamed. "You're fitting us up. It's against…"

"I know," Doug interrupted. "It's against your human rights. Give it a rest."

They were handcuffed while screaming obscenities and accusations.

Doug knew he had left sufficient drugs so they couldn't just claim it was for personal use. They would be prosecuted for dealing and were certain to receive a jail sentence.

The drugs would be deposited in the property room back at the police station, which was exactly where they had been until the previous evening. He'd signed them out and returned them an hour later, except what he returned was baking powder. The original case for which they were evidence had concluded and the drugs were shortly to have been incinerated.

Working for the regional organised crime unit, he had constant access to a supply of drugs and was finally making some real money by supplying Scott.

However, he couldn't keep dipping into the property room and the doubling of Scott's order would require him to find other routes to source his product. He was already working on a solution to the problem. He knew who supplied most of the dealers in Sussex. Doug was going to set up a meeting and offer his services in exchange for supplies at a good price.

Powell had an uneventful day. At lunch, Scott invited him to sit next to him and thanked him for helping Hattie, at the supermarket. Tommy looked irked at being pushed from his normal seat as he made room for Powell to sit down.

Scott asked Powell a variety of questions about his past. Powell recognised Scott was probing, trying to find out more about him but he was subtle and pleasant in his manner. Powell managed to ask a few questions of his own but Scott was very good at avoiding answering. They played a game of ping pong with their questions, neither of them learning anything really useful about the other.

At dinner, Powell returned to his seat in the middle of the table and quickly found Carol and Kirsty to each side.

"Hope you don't mind us joining you?" Kirsty asked. "We saw you mixing with the elite end of the table at lunch."

"And you want to know why I was sitting next to Scott?"

"Are we that obvious?" Carol asked. "Not much different happens around here from day to day. We girls need something to gossip about."

"I'm sorry but this isn't worth gossiping about. Scott thanked me for helping Hattie with the shopping yesterday and then just asked me how I was settling in. I told him everything was going well and I found you two especially helpful."

"Now you're taking the piss," Carol replied.

Powell held his hands up in the air in mock surrender. "Okay. I didn't specifically mention you but I said everyone was making me feel very welcome."

"How are you getting on with solving the meaning of life?" Kirsty asked.

"Slow progress," Powell admitted.

The conversation remained light throughout the rest of dinner. They carried their plates to the kitchen and Powell helped wash up as it was his designated turn.

On the way back to the lounge, he encountered Carol in the hallway, having an animated conversation with Tommy. Powell stood back for a moment, not wanting to interfere. He saw Tommy take her by the arm and it was evident Carol wasn't happy.

"Hi guys," Powell said cheerfully, as he approached. "What's the plan for the rest of the evening?"

"Get lost," Tommy replied.

"That's not very friendly. And you look as if you're hurting Carol. Please let go of her arm."

"I told you to get lost," Tommy replied, letting go of Carol's arm and turning to face Powell. He puffed out his considerable chest and stared Powell in the eyes. "Is there something wrong with your hearing?"

"Carol, do you want to go play some table tennis?" Powell asked, completely ignoring Tommy.

"She's going upstairs with me," Tommy answered. "Now piss off before I forget you're new."

Carol took a step closer to Tommy and linked arms. "We're wasting time here," she said. A small nod in Powell's direction was telling him not to interfere.

Tommy smiled at her, obviously pleased by her change of attitude. "Looks like you will have to find yourself a new ping pong partner."

"You don't have to go with him if you don't want to," Powell stressed.

"Of course she bloody wants to go with me," Tommy answered. "Learn to mind your own business."

Carol tugged on Tommy's arm. "Let's go."

Powell moved out of the way as the two of them walked past and ignored Tommy's smug grin. He was fairly sure Carol was only going with Tommy to avoid trouble. She probably thought she was saving Powell from being on the wrong end of Tommy's fists.

CHAPTER NINE

Powell returned from his morning run and after his shower, went down to breakfast. He immediately looked for Carol and found her sitting alone in the dining room. Even at a distance, he could see the beginnings of a black eye. He was pleased there was no sign of Tommy.

"Can I get you some more coffee," Powell asked, spotting her empty cup and deliberately avoiding the subject of her eye.

"Thanks," Carol replied with a smile. "Black, please. Like my eye. Don't pretend you didn't notice it."

Powell was surprised by her good humour. He poured two coffees and then sat beside her.

"Sorry about last night," Carol apologised after tasting her coffee. "I shouldn't have got you involved."

"I got myself involved. What happened to your eye?"

"Walked into a cupboard. Careless of me."

"I don't believe you."

"You need to be careful," Carol warned. "Tommy can be a mean son of a bitch."

"Then why did you leave with him last night?"

"I owed him."

"What does that mean?"

"He gets me my supplies but unlike some of the people here, I have to pay for everything. I'm behind with my payments so Tommy told me it was time to pay up and as I don't have any money right now…"

"He blackmailed you into having sex with him?"

"That sounds more dramatic than the reality. I've fucked him before so it wasn't really a big deal."

"I had the distinct impression if I hadn't come along you would have refused to go with him."

"That was a little too much weed giving me some false courage. You don't want to say *No* to Tommy. Actually, I'm grateful you came along because it made me see sense. He would have hurt me far more if I hadn't seen sense."

"So the black eye is his doing?"

"Please stay out of this," Carol implored. "I can handle Tommy."

"Really? I'm not sure how him thumping you rates as handling him. How is the rest of your body. Have you any more cuts or bruises I can't see?"

"Not really."

"Not really? What does that mean? How did he hurt you?"

"Only the way some men like to when they have sex."

Powell didn't want to force Carol to answer any more of his questions. He'd learned enough. "Are you okay now?" he asked. "Do you need a doctor?"

"I'm fine and thanks for asking. Everyone else around here is scared to death of Tommy and runs a mile at the mere mention of his name."

Powell knew it was only a matter of time before he and Tommy would come to blows. Powell couldn't stand bullies but especially men who mistreated women.

"Does Scott know what Tommy is like?"

"Of course. Tommy doesn't shit without Scott's approval."

"So why do you stay?"

"I've been anorexic, bulimic, done far too many drugs and even self-harmed when I was a teenager. I've had one very screwed up life but the funny thing is, I've done none of those things since living here. Well apart from smoking a joint whenever I want one but that doesn't count as it's almost medicinal. I'm well fed and if I wasn't living here, I'd be working on a checkout at Asda and living in a crappy squat somewhere, probably doing heroin."

"So how do you pay to live here?"

"At first Scott didn't want any money. He just enjoyed my company and everything was great. Then Hattie came along and that all changed. Be careful of her, she's not the sweet and innocent girl she portrays. She soon had her claws into Scott and I was history."

"So how do you get by now?"

"I make deliveries for him and in return he gives me a little money and I get to stay."

"What type of deliveries?"

"I don't look inside the parcels."

"That won't be an adequate defence if you end up in Court."

"Look Powell, I shouldn't be telling you all this. You seem like a decent guy so if I was you, I'd get the hell out of here, first chance you get."

"Thanks for the advice. I'm not planning to spend too long here. I just want to get my head straight. There's been a lot happening in my life over the last couple of years."

"Well be careful and stay clear of Tommy. He used to be in the army. He's been to Afghanistan and when he's drunk, he tells stories about how they used to amuse themselves cutting up the locals. After last night, I wouldn't be surprised if you've made an enemy of him and Tommy is not someone you want as your enemy."

Powell smiled reassuringly. "I've handled worse than Tommy."

Carol raised her eyebrows in surprise. "I'd like to hear those stories sometime."

"When do you make your deliveries?" Powell asked. "Is it a regular time and place?"

"Why do you want to know? Are you planning to rob me?" Carol looked genuinely concerned. "Tommy will kill me if I mess up one of his deliveries."

"Don't worry, I promise I'm not going to rob you. It's just that's the only time you leave the house. If I had something I needed delivering, would you do it for me? I'd pay you for your help.

"It depends where it is and what it is," Carol asked suspiciously.

"It would be a message. Tell me where you go and I'll arrange for my friend to collect the message. I'd be willing to pay you a couple of hundred pounds each time and I'll give you two hundred now as an advance."

"Two hundred pounds to deliver a message? Must be a very important message."

"I may never need you but it's good to know the option exists."

"My regular trip is on a Wednesday afternoon. I take a parcel into Crawley."

"What time approximately?"

"I have to be at the café in Tilgate Park at three in the afternoon. I sit and order a coffee and we exchange bags."

Powell took two hundred pounds from his wallet. "Here you are. I don't expect the money back, even if I never use your services."

"Thanks," Carol replied, quickly pushing the money into her jeans pocket.

"If I can help in any way, don't hesitate to ask," Powell offered. "Especially if Tommy bothers you again."

"Thanks, Powell. And similarly, if I can ever do anything for you, be sure to ask." She smiled and winked suggestively. Then added more seriously, "Even if you just need someone to talk to. It can get quite lonely here. If I didn't have Kirsty, I'd go mad."

"I might take you up on your offer… of a chat." Powell smiled, knowing he had teased her for a second.

"You do that. Now I need to get to work. I'm on potato peeling duty this morning."

CHAPTER TEN

As the morning passed, Powell tried to keep an eye on the front lawn, waiting for the right moment. He had jobs to complete and handyman Dave was becoming quite a taskmaster.

"What the hell outside is so interesting?" Dave asked, after he caught Powell yet again peering out the window.

"Sorry. I was checking the weather."

"Well it won't have changed much since the last time you checked, about five minutes ago. Nor since the other ten times you've checked this morning."

Powell was keeping half an eye on the weather, hoping the rain would stay away. Tommy regularly went outside for a cigarette break but not if it was raining. Powell wanted to get Tommy on his own and the first couple of times he watched Tommy go outside, he had fellow smokers for company.

"Sorry, Dave. I was watching everyone going for a cigarette. I was hoping to grab a moment with Carol."

"You smitten by her?"

"A little."

"Better keep watching out then. I can finish the next couple of jobs by myself."

"Thanks, Dave."

"No problem. You've been a huge help since you joined us. I was getting fed up of working by myself."

"I owe you a beer."

"And I'm not averse to a beer or two. Good luck with Carol. She's a nice girl."

The opportunity Powell wanted, finally presented itself as lunch was approaching. He hurried downstairs and out the front door.

Tommy gave Powell a contemptuous stare as he noticed him approach. "You a smoker?" he asked.

"No. Didn't anyone ever tell you it's bad for your health."

"What do you want then if you're not a smoker?"

"I wanted a word with you."

"Well I don't want to speak to you so get lost."

Powell stopped in front of Tommy. "Why was Carol bruised and cut this morning?"

"Perhaps she had a fall. She can be a clumsy cow sometimes."

"Did you hit her?"

"It's none of your fucking business. Go back inside unless you want some of the same."

"So you did hit her?"

"Didn't you hear me," Tommy threatened, throwing the remains of his cigarette on the ground and crushing it with the heel of his shoe. "You might be able to scare off a couple of drug addicts but I'm a different kettle of fish."

"And you won't find it as easy to hit me as Carol."

"You think so?" Tommy asked and immediately looked to throw a punch with his right hand.

Powell was pleased Tommy was so predictable. He was on the balls of his feet and easily moved to his right to avoid the punch. The punch had been a feint and Tommy delivered the real punch with a left to Powell's midriff. Tommy had a considerable weight behind the punch and Powell grunted and bent over.

The follow up punch caught him on the side of the face but Powell had been expecting it and was able to ride the punch. He collapsed to the ground.

"That wasn't very difficult," Tommy sneered. "I'd stay down there if you don't want more."

"Why would you hit a woman?" Powell asked, clutching his stomach and showing no inclination to get up.

"Because I fucking wanted to hurt her," Tommy snarled. "She deserved it for messing me around. Anyway, a girl like Carol enjoys it rough. She likes being with a real man. She didn't complain."

"I'm sure she didn't. Otherwise, you would, no doubt, have hit her some more. Carol's not stupid. But I have to tell you, hitting a defenceless woman doesn't make you a real man. Quite the opposite. You're an apology for a man. You want to keep off those steroids. They pickle your brain."

"You aren't so bright yourself, picking a fight with me," Tommy answered, advancing on Powell. "You'll be taking your meals through a straw after I've finished with you."

Powell was prepared. In one motion, he sprung off the floor into a crouch. Tommy came to a stop, surprised by Powell's sudden movement.

"I just wanted to hear confirmation from your lips that you had hit Carol," Powell explained. "I let you put me on the ground for a minute and you think it's all over. You're obviously too used to hitting women. I'm rather more resilient."

Powell didn't want to get in close with the larger Tommy, who though more of a brawler than a trained fighter, would be a dangerous brawler. Tommy had raised his hands in front of his face like a boxer expecting a fist fight. He took two steps towards Powell and again threw a punch with his right fist but this time it wasn't a feint.

Powell crouched, turned his back under the punch and then spun back with an outstretched foot. The spinning heel kick connected with Tommy's ankles, resulting in him losing balance. He was deposited on the ground before he knew what had happened.

"All those muscles aren't much use if you move as slow as a cart horse," Powell laughed.

Powell was happy to see a shaken Tommy quickly on his feet. He had every intention of teaching Tommy a lesson, he wouldn't forget. Powell had been taught to strike fast and end a fight before it really got started but he intended to go against all his training.

He didn't want a quick end to this fight. He was angry inside and needed an outlet for his feelings. Tommy was a bully and there was nothing Powell hated more than a bully. It needed someone to stand up to a bully and Powell had nominated himself for the job.

Tommy circled Powell, wary of getting too close. Powell adopted his fighting stance but with his hands down by his sides, inviting Tommy to come forward.

Powell was preparing for Tommy's next assault when his concentration was broken by the sound of Scott shouting, "Stop fighting." Out the corner of his eye, Powell could see Scott hurrying in their direction.

Neither man showed any indication of having heard Scott and kept circling each other. Powell kept his eyes fixed firmly on Tommy, who he felt was certain to take advantage of any diversion.

"Stop this," Scott demanded, as he reached the two fighters. "You're causing a scene. Everyone is watching."

Powell glanced towards the house and saw a small group had gathered on the steps. He remained alert but adopted a more relaxed stance. "Tommy seems to think it's okay to beat up Carol."

"Did she tell you that?" Scott asked.

Powell didn't want to get her in more trouble. "No but you only have to see her bruised face to know what he did."

Tommy had stopped circling and was standing with his hands on his hips.

"How do you know it was Tommy?" Scott probed.

"He just admitted it," Powell replied.

"It was just a bit of rough sex," Tommy explained. "Carol enjoys it rough."

"Bollocks," Powell swore. "Tell Tommy to keep away from Carol or next time you'll be calling him an ambulance. This is a final warning."

"If Carol has a complaint against Tommy, she must bring it to me," Scott stated, raising his voice. "Powell, we don't tolerate fighting. If you have a problem, you come to me with it. We don't settle arguments with our fists."

"Sorry," Powell apologised. "It won't happen again." He didn't want to get kicked out of the commune. If it came down to a choice, Scott would undoubtedly support Tommy.

As Powell turned and walked towards the house, Tommy called out, "This isn't finished."

CHAPTER ELEVEN

Hattie arranged to meet her mother at a tea room in Haywards Heath. Her mother had quickly accepted Hattie's invitation, she was so pleased and relieved to finally hear from her daughter. Hattie stressed she didn't want to see her father. She wished just to talk to her mother.

"How are you?" Clara enquired, once they were seated. "Is everything okay at that place?"

"I'm fine," Hattie answered. "Why must you talk about where I live like it was dog shit?"

"Must you swear?"

"Dad always swears. You never tell him to stop."

"It's different. It's unbecoming for a young woman to use profanity."

"But it's all right for men to swear? Honestly mum, your ideas are prehistoric. Women can do anything men can do."

"I'd prefer for neither of you to swear."

"Look, I don't want to argue," Hattie stressed. "I came here hoping you were getting used to the idea of where I live and accepting my adult right to make decisions about my life." Receiving no immediate response she added, "Even if you don't like my decisions."

"We're just worried for you."

"Well don't be. I love what I'm doing. Life is great at Tintagel."

"We don't want them to take advantage of you."

"Mum, it's a long time since I was a virgin."

"I don't mean that way. We're worried about what you might do with your inheritance."

Hattie stared at her mother in disbelief for a few seconds. "Do you honestly think I'd give away all my inheritance? Do you really think

I'm that stupid?"

Before Clara could answer, their coffee and cakes were delivered.

"We don't know what to think," Clara answered, once the waitress had left. "You run away to join a cult and you told me you were having sex with Scott, who must be twice your age. Then you admit you're taking drugs. How do you expect me to react? Especially when you don't answer your phone."

"Firstly, it is not a cult and I didn't run anywhere. I took a train and a taxi. We are living as a commune. It's completely different to a cult. Secondly, when it comes to sex, I happen to prefer older men. They know what they're doing. Finally, and most importantly, I have no intention of handing over my inheritance to Scott or anyone else."

Clara sighed with relief. "That's good to hear."

"Perhaps now you can tell Dad to call off whoever it is he has poking around asking questions about where I live."

"Actually it was me who found him, not your father."

"So it's true? You really have hired some form of private investigator?"

"He came highly recommended," Clara admitted, wondering if she should have just denied everything. But she didn't want to lie to her daughter. For the first time in ages, they were having a proper conversation. "I'm sorry. I was getting desperate and didn't know what else to do."

"Promise me you will get rid of him," Hattie demanded. "As you can see, I am perfectly okay. It's embarrassing having my mother pay someone to check up on me."

Clara was feeling guilty. She should have had more belief in her daughter. Hattie may not have been interested in the academic side of school but she was no fool. Clara should have trusted her not to behave stupidly. Instead, Clara had been the one to behave stupidly and hired someone to spy on her daughter. What had she been thinking?

"I'm sorry," Clara repeated. "I was just so worried about you. Frankly, I'm still worried but I guess I have to recognise you're no longer our little girl. You've grown up."

"I still love you," Hattie stressed. "But I need to make my own decisions and I might make some mistakes but that's life."

"You know, it's not easy being a parent. For eighteen years of your life you worry every day about your daughter and then suddenly she's an adult and you are expected to press a button and stop worrying."

Hattie reached forward and took her mother's hand in her own. "You can still worry about me but you have to treat me like an adult. You can't snoop in my bag or go hiring private investigators."

Clara nodded in agreement. "I'm so glad you called me," she said, perking up. "I'd been really missing you."

"We should do this more often. I promise I'll call you at least once a week."

"That would be nice."

"So tell me about this private investigator. I've never met one in real life. What's he like?"

"I've only met Powell once but he seems very nice. Angela Bennett worships him."

Hattie was momentarily lost for words. "Powell is the man you hired?"

CHAPTER TWELVE

Powell was pleased to accept Hattie's suggestion to accompany her shopping. The more time he spent with her, the better for his investigations. He also felt a duty to protect her and if the two drug addicts turned up again, she could be in danger.

He was beginning to discover a darker side to life at the house. Carol had pointed the finger at Hattie, accusing her of being part of Scott's inner circle, which by default implicated her in the drug dealing. Of course, there was the possibility Carol was acting out of jealousy, blaming Hattie for taking her place in Scott's bed.

However, the evidence Hattie was involved with drug dealing was starting to stack up. Powell had seen first-hand, Hattie pass drugs to Lucy in the pub and she'd admitted providing drugs to the two addicts in the supermarket car park. Powell was fairly confident she wasn't a big user herself but in the eyes of the police, dealing was a far bigger crime than smoking a little weed.

Powell enjoyed the idea of getting away from the house, even if it was only a trip to the supermarket, which in itself seemed slightly absurd. How his life had changed in a very short time, if he found the idea of going food shopping exciting!

At Tintagel, he felt cut off from the rest of the world. He hadn't realised how much he would miss having his phone and computer, even for what was so far a relatively short time. Within the next couple of days, he was going to have to find a way to place a call to Hattie's mother and give her an update. He imagined her sitting by the phone, desperate for news.

The longer Powell spent at Tintagel, the more concerned he became for Hattie's safety. There was an undercurrent of friction in the house between different members of the commune. On the surface, everyone smiled but underneath, there was the full range of human emotions on display, including plenty of anger and jealousy.

Hattie probably thought she was in control of her life but Powell suspected, Scott could be quite manipulative. They seemed very close but whether they had anything approaching a serious relationship was impossible to tell. It could well be a relationship based on physical desire and convenience. It certainly wasn't an exclusive relationship. Hattie had made it very clear she would sleep with Powell if he was interested.

It appeared Scott had involved Hattie with his drug business, in the same way he used Carol. Powell believed Scott was behind Hattie selling drugs in the pub and to the addicts at the supermarket. It was an indicator of the influence Scott exerted. What Powell didn't yet know, was how deeply Hattie was involved in Scott's business.

Powell believed drugs and violence were never far apart, which had been proved on their previous trip to the supermarket. If he hadn't been present, Hattie could have been stabbed. Powell felt he had good reason to be worried for her safety.

Tommy was a particularly loose cannon, who spelled potential danger to anyone who crossed his path. Powell had made an enemy for life and would have to be on his guard. If Hattie was Scott's favourite, then Tommy would hopefully have the sense to steer clear of her, rather than risk upsetting his employer.

Tintagel was definitely not a place Powell would have wanted Bella to live and he would have dragged her away kicking and screaming if necessary. Fortunately, his daughter had not been the type of girl to want to join a commune. She had joined the police because she wanted to help other people. She didn't want to run away from life. Powell felt great sympathy for Clara Buckingham's situation. She undoubtedly loved her daughter but was powerless to effect change. Powell wanted to help but also wanted to keep within the law.

Powell found it difficult to fathom why someone like Hattie, with all her advantages in life, would want to live at Tintagel. In truth, he resented her a little for the way she chose to live her life. It may not always have been easy at home but she had wanted for nothing. It sounded a better upbringing than his own boarding school education.

She was in danger of wasting her life while Bella's life had been cut so short. Advice columns would probably say it wasn't that unusual for Hattie to want to rebel against her privileged upbringing. If she wanted to escape her parents, why couldn't she go abroad and work in a refugee camp, doing something useful?

On many levels, Powell liked Hattie but she was making the wrong decisions in life. Who was he kidding? In his youth, he'd made decisions that now seemed completely inappropriate. His wrong decisions had led to the death of his wife and a multitude of other regrets.

He believed, the wrong decisions shape your life more than the right decisions. The lessons you learn from the wrong decisions, equip you to go forward in life and use experience to make better decisions in the future. Some people do keep repeating the same mistakes but he wasn't generally one of them.

Hattie was no different to most other people her age. She was looking for answers to the same questions every generation tried to answer. Perhaps it was a phase she would grow out of but Powell wanted to ensure she had the opportunity to come out the other side, both in one piece and not broke.

Whatever her feelings today, there would probably come a time when she would look back on her young life and regret the worst of her foolishness. Hattie was playing with fire by living at the commune rather than living it up in Mayfair and Chelsea.

Powell was driving his own BMW to the supermarket this time as the Land Rover was being used by someone else. Hattie had promised it was a smaller shop than their previous trip so they would be able to fit everything into his car.

It wasn't much more than a country lane from Tintagel to the outskirts of Haywards Heath town centre so he didn't drive fast. Hattie seemed less chatty than usual and rather withdrawn, which she explained was due to tiredness. Powell resisted the urge to bombard her with questions and it was a relatively quiet journey.

After less than an hour shopping, Powell emerged from the supermarket with a full trolley. Hattie was carrying an additional bag and between them they had a week's supply of food for the commune.

He was pleased there was no sign of the two crackheads, who had caused trouble last time. Perhaps they had learned their lesson. Although, they didn't seem like the type who would learn from their mistakes and would almost certainly spend their life repeating their mistakes.

As Powell approached the car, an instinct told him something was wrong. Something didn't feel right. The car park seemed eerily quiet. Where were the other shoppers?

He was still trying to analyse exactly what was the problem, when he suddenly found himself surrounded by police officers barking instructions. They had literally jumped out from everywhere.

They all had their arms extended and were holding guns, which were gripped in both hands and pointing at his body. Powell was extremely nervous as he knew how easily a wrong movement could be interpreted.

He hoped these were experienced officers. They had caught him by surprise and he was completely surrounded. There was no escape, not that he had any intention of running anywhere. He hadn't committed any crime.

Powell placed his hands high in the air and watched as the shopping trolley slowly rolled forward into his very new BMW. He had to fight to control the urge to grab the trolley. Any sudden move on his part wouldn't be appreciated by the armed police.

Two officers shouted at him to get on the ground and he did as instructed, careful to keep his hands in full view. He could see Hattie doing the same. He said nothing as the handcuffs were applied. They wouldn't be the people to provide answers. He was gripped firmly by each arm and helped to stand. Then an officer carefully started searching him but there was nothing to find.

Whatever the reason for his current predicament, he knew it wasn't for something small like an unpaid fine. They didn't send armed response units to collect payment for parking tickets. Whatever they thought he had done, they had been concerned he might be armed and dangerous.

He suspected he could be in a bundle of trouble but he believed everything would be sorted out down the police station. He just needed to remain calm. There was no point in shouting out his innocence.

Out the corner of his eye, he saw a policeman unlock his car with the keys taken from his pocket. A few seconds later, the same officer stepped back from the car with a bag of white powder in his hand and held it up for all to see.

It hit Powell like a blow to the solar plexus. A more powerful blow in fact than he had experienced in most of his kick boxing training. He glanced at Hattie but she was already being bundled into the back of a police car.

An officer in plain clothes approached Powell and went through the formality of arresting him and reading him his rights. Powell chose to remain silent.

As they pushed him into the back of a police car, he started thinking about what had gone wrong. One thing seemed certain. The Land Rover had been unavailable so he had been forced to take his own car. That surely wasn't just a coincidence. Scott or one of his henchmen must have placed the drugs in his car. They would only do that if they knew his real purpose for joining the commune.

What he didn't know was whether Hattie had been part of the trap. Had she placed the drugs in the car? He didn't think it was likely because she had also been arrested.

CHAPTER THIRTEEN

At the police station, Powell was brought before the custody Sergeant, who stood behind a circular, raised desk. Powell confirmed his name and address and was thoroughly searched again by a different officer, than at the supermarket. A further officer stood close by, presumably in case Powell showed any signs of causing trouble.

Powell handed over his few valuables to the sergeant, who placed them in a bag. They then asked him for his belt and checked his shoes but he was wearing a pair without laces. They obviously didn't want him hanging himself in his cell. The bag was sealed and Powell signed a receipt.

He was asked if he wanted to speak to a solicitor and declined, asking instead for Brian, his friend in the security services, to be informed of his arrest, although he didn't bother to mention the security services connection. The police wouldn't take kindly to any perceived interference from that direction.

Powell provided Brian's number, who Powell was confident would be able to provide more help than any local solicitor. When a solicitor was needed, Brian would be able to recommend someone good.

Powell then had his finger prints taken and a DNA sample taken by putting a swab in his mouth. He was conscious that the results would sit on a database for eternity. It made him feel uncomfortable and vulnerable. Formalities over, he was escorted to a cell.

There had been no sign of Hattie at the police station, which was surprising and slightly disconcerting. Why wasn't she being put in a cell? The most likely answer was that she was considered an innocent witness, not a suspect. It was his car and she was just accompanying him on a shopping trip. She hadn't even known him very long. It sounded like a story that would be easy for the police to believe.

After two hours in the cold cell, he was shown to a small, windowless interview room with a cheap metal table in the middle. The walls were originally white but had turned a shade of grey with time. The lighting was provided by a flickering, fluorescent strip. The room was depressing and cold, which was probably intentional.

He was sat in a chair on one side of the table. Two further chairs sat empty on the other side of the table. It was a strange feeling, remembering the many interviews of suspects, he'd carried out in Northern Ireland. He'd been sitting on the other side of the table in those days.

Powell was left to his own thoughts for twenty minutes, almost certainly a ploy to instil nervousness in the guilty but he wasn't guilty and there would be no confession.

Two men eventually entered the room and sat down. Powell remained silent. He wasn't going to be the first to speak.

The man wearing a suit turned on the tape recorder, which sat on the table. His colleague was wearing jeans and an open necked, check shirt.

"I'm Detective Inspector Bates and this is Sergeant Willis," the suit said. He recorded the date and time of the interview. "Please state your full name, date of birth and current address."

Powell did as instructed, giving his home address.

"I understand you have declined legal advice," Bates continued, mostly for the benefit of the recording. He didn't want any case going down the pan on a technicality. "Has it been explained to you that this is free and you need not answer any questions without a solicitor present?"

"I don't need a solicitor. I haven't committed any crime."

"Then would you mind explaining to me why we found a large bag of what we suspect to be cocaine, hidden in your car?"

"I have no idea how it came to be there. I've never seen it before."

"It will go much easier on you in court if you help us," Bates urged. "Tell us where you got the drugs and I'll put in a good word to the judge."

"You're not listening to me. They aren't my drugs."

"Then how do you explain them being in your car?"

"I have no idea how they came to be in my car. I only know I've never seen them before."

"Look Powell, don't give me that nonsense. The drugs haven't magically transported themselves to your car."

"I can see why they made you a detective."

Bates continued, completely unfazed by the sarcasm. "You gave your home address earlier as somewhere in Hove. But I understood you were living at Tintagel, a commune near Lindfield."

"I was staying there temporarily to see if I liked the place. Given today's events, I think it's safe to assume I won't be returning."

"So are you trying to tell me that someone else at this commune, where you've been living, has planted the drugs in your car?" Bates quizzed.

"You work it out. You're the detective."

"Would you care to enlighten me with the name of who you suspect of putting the drugs in your car? And why they put them there?"

"Without wanting to sound repetitive, you're the detective."

"I am the detective and currently I have what appears to be a watertight case."

"Your case is like a colander. For a start, I assume you received an anonymous tip off that there were drugs in my car. Secondly, there was another person in the car. Thirdly, my fingerprints are not on the bag containing the drugs. Doesn't that strike you as odd?"

"We haven't yet run fingerprint analysis on the bag."

"Well you won't be finding my prints because I've never seen that bag before, let alone touched it."

"Tip offs are common in my line of work, especially when a dealer wants to get rid of his competition."

There was a knock at the door, a man in plain clothes entered, walked up to Bates and whispered something in his ear.

"This interview is suspended at 2.56 pm," Bates announced into the recorder, climbing to his feet. He nodded for his Sergeant to follow him and hurried to the door.

Powell was concerned. What had been so important? Perhaps Brian had arrived at the police station, revealed he worked for the security services and was making a nuisance of himself. Hopefully, Bates had been summoned to hear he was interviewing someone, who definitely wasn't a drug dealer. Powell had an uneasy feeling in his stomach, which cast doubt on that idea.

CHAPTER FOURTEEN

Powell didn't have to wait long for the two officers to return. He studied their faces as they entered the room but could detect no reason for feeling positive.

Bates turned the recording machine back on and restated the time and who was present.

"I've just been informed that a search of your car has revealed a hand gun hidden in the boot of your car," Bates continued. "I have to ask you again at this point, whether you would like to have legal representation?"

Powell realised the Inspector was protecting his arse. Making sure he had on record that he had offered. He didn't want his case thrown out on a technicality at some later date.

Powell replied clearly, "I have done nothing wrong so don't require legal representation."

Bates took a photo from his folder and pushed it across the table towards Powell. "I am now showing Powell a picture of the gun found in the boot of his car, earlier today."

Powell glanced at the photo expecting the worst and wasn't disappointed. The photo showed a gun in the small compartment where the tools for changing a wheel were kept.

"Do you have a permit for this gun?" Bates asked.

"I have never seen this gun before. It's not mine so obviously, I don't have a permit."

"Do you keep your car locked when you're not using it?"

"Yes."

"Was your car locked when you went to it this morning?"

Powell pretended to think about it for a minute but knew the answer immediately. "Yes, it was locked." He was remembering how the keys were left in the pocket of his jacket, hanging in a cupboard where he was sleeping. Anyone could help themselves to the keys and he would be none the wiser, which is exactly what had happened.

"But you want us to believe someone else has gained access to your car and planted the drugs and weapon?"

"My keys were in my jacket pocket, hanging in my room at Tintagel. It would have been quite possible for someone to borrow the keys, plant the gun and then return the keys to my pocket. That would be my explanation for what must have happened."

"And who exactly would do this?"

"It was probably the same person who provided the tip off and must have mentioned, I may have a weapon. Otherwise, you wouldn't have used all those armed officers to arrest me."

"The gun has been sent for ballistic tests. If it has been used in any crime, we will find out."

"I'm sure you will but even if it has been used in a crime, it wasn't used by me. I've never seen it before."

"If you are going to continue with this stance, I am going to bring this interview to an end for the time being," Bates said. "Do you have anything else to say?"

"As you will have discovered, I have no criminal record. However, I am well known to the police in Brighton. I can think of at least a couple of senior offices, who will vouch for my good character. Last year my daughter, who was a very new constable, was murdered while on duty in the town centre."

"That's where I know you from," Willis interjected, speaking for the first time. "I saw you at the funeral. I knew Bella."

"I'm sorry about your daughter," Bates said sympathetically. "I know the loss of a loved one can be a terrible blow. Have you been struggling to cope? Has it led to you getting involved with drugs?"

"The two things are not connected. I've not had some form of breakdown and turned to drugs."

"It would be understandable if you had," Bates persisted. "Is that why you joined the commune? To get away from everything? I'm sure a judge would be lenient, given your history."

Powell drew a deep breath. "My history, as you put it, has nothing to do with my joining the commune." He hesitated, uncertain about giving the real reasons for his joining the commune. "I met Scott and Hattie in a pub and they suggested, I pay a visit. It sounded like a good idea at the time."

"And what is your *relationship* to Hattie?" Bates asked and the way he emphasised the word relationship, was hinting at something beyond friendship.

"We both live at the commune and I was helping her with the shopping. It's the second time I've gone along to help her with carrying the bags. Everyone at Tintagel has to share the chores."

"Do you think she put the drugs in the car?"

"I have no idea." Powell was in a quandary. He was being paid to help Hattie not get her arrested for dealing in drugs. "Have you arrested Hattie?"

"She's being interviewed at the moment," Willis answered.

Bates gave his junior partner a withering look. "We'll ask the questions, Powell."

Powell was fed up of being on the defensive. "Sometime soon you are going to receive a phone call, telling you I must have been framed. It will come from someone very senior in the security services." Powell suddenly had both men's attention. "I know it will piss you off that they are interfering but I used to work for them and they will vouch for me."

For the first time, Powell noticed a look of uncertainty on the face of Bates. He leaned forward and switched off the recorder before demanding, "What the fuck's going on here?"

"I told you. I'm being framed."

"Do you work for the security services?" Bates asked.

"Not for a long time."

"Then why would they be able to vouch for you?"

"Because I've been of help to them quite recently."

"I don't suppose you would want to explain how you helped the security services?"

"Let's just say it was in an unofficial capacity and I helped find the terrorists responsible for the bombing of the Brighton centre."

Willis raised his eyebrows and looked at his boss but this time said nothing. Bates gave Powell a long and thoughtful stare without saying anything. Powell met his gaze without blinking.

Bates turned the recorder back on. "I am temporarily suspending this interview." He gave the time and stood up. "We will talk again soon."

Powell assumed Bates was intending to do some more digging on his background before they spoke again. At least he had given Bates some food for thought.

Powell knew they were going to have to put him in front of a magistrate within twenty four hours. Given the evidence against him, he recognised he was unlikely to be given bail. The amount of drugs went far beyond what could be explained away, as for personal use.

He didn't fancy being locked up for weeks waiting for a trial. He needed to be free to find whoever was responsible for his current problems. He couldn't do that from inside a jail. Brian's boss owed him a favour and it was time to collect.

CHAPTER FIFTEEN

Powell was relieved when he walked out of court. The prosecution had not contested the request for bail and he knew that was largely down to Brian's influence. It had helped that he had a clean record and owned a bar in Brighton, which made the risk of him fleeing, less likely.

Powell had noticed Bates sitting in court and he looked like he'd chewed a very bitter lemon when the Magistrate granted bail. In truth, the agreement regarding bail had been made before they ever came to court. With Brian's help, he had called in the favour owed by the Director General of MI5. A word in the right ear had ensured Powell was free at least until his case came to court in a few weeks.

Powell had learned that Hattie was not charged with any crime. It was Powell's car and she had simply been a passenger, professing to be completely unaware of the weapon or drugs. Exactly what he thought she would say and it was probably the truth, although he couldn't be certain she wasn't involved in his arrest. He decided that the first thing he needed to do, was to visit Hattie's parents.

A couple of hours after leaving the court he was on a train to London. His car was still being held by the police so he was going to have to hire a replacement but that could wait.

"I've been trying to get hold of you," Clara said impatiently, as the maid showed him into the lounge.

Powell ordered coffee and sat in an armchair. "I've only just seen the missed calls," he explained. "I didn't have my phone with me the last few days."

"Why ever not?"

"It's a long story and I'll tell you it in a minute. Why were you so keen to speak with me?"

"I've spoken with Harriet and to be honest, I now regret ever having asked you to help."

"Why is that?"

"I should have trusted Harriet not to do anything stupid. She was really upset I hired you."

"You told her about me?"

"Well she knew someone had been asking questions and I told her, I was responsible for hiring you, not her father."

How did Hattie know someone was asking questions? He'd been keeping a very low profile and didn't believe he'd been guilty of asking too many questions. The only other person asking questions was Brian and he would have been very discrete. Something didn't add up.

"Did you by any chance mention my name?" Powell asked.

"I did. I hope you don't mind?"

Powell chose his words carefully. "It might have been better if you hadn't given Hattie my name."

"What do you mean?"

Powell explained the events of the last twenty four hours, stopping only briefly when the maid brought in the coffee.

Clara was shocked by Powell's revelations. "But surely you don't think your arrest is anything to do with Harriet?"

"What would you think in my place? She never mentioned to me that she knew I was working for you. Don't you think that's strange?"

"It's an absurd notion. Where would Harriet get those type of drugs or a gun?"

Powell decided it was time for some straight talking. "All types of drugs are freely available at the house. I've even seen Hattie sell some to the barmaid at the local pub."

"But why would she sell drugs? She doesn't need the money."

"She may have just been doing someone a favour. I don't know."

"Have you seen Harriet taking drugs?" Clara asked, obviously concerned. "She promised me she wasn't."

"She might be taking a little, virtually everyone at the house does, but if you are asking me whether she's addicted to something like cocaine, then I think I can answer that I saw no sign of any addiction or even heavy use."

"Thank God!"

"As for the gun, perhaps it came from Scott. He has a former soldier working for him and I wouldn't be surprised if he had access to guns. I don't know for certain but I am fairly confident that when you told Hattie about me, she would have told Scott."

"That must be it. Scott is responsible not Harriet."

Powell wasn't impressed Clara didn't seem to care about the trouble she had caused him, only that the blame could be laid at Scott's feet not Hattie's. If Clara hadn't mentioned his name to Hattie, he was fairly confident he wouldn't now be in such a mess with the law. There was no point in having a go at Clara and pointing out client confidentiality was a two way street. It was water under the bridge.

"Anyway," Powell continued. "I came here to update you on recent events and tell you I can't work for you anymore. I have to try and clear my name and I think there may be a conflict of interest."

"Could it be someone else, nothing to do with the commune, who planted the drugs and gun?" Clara asked.

"It could be but frankly, I think it's very unlikely. The only chance anyone had to plant the drugs or gun was while my car was parked at Tintagel."

"I'm sorry," Clara apologised. "This is all my fault. I never should have involved you in my family problems."

"It isn't your fault," Powell stressed. "You didn't plant anything in my car. And I didn't have to accept the job in the first place so don't go blaming yourself."

"What are you going to do?"

"Find out who is responsible for this mess."

"How can I help?"

"I haven't told the police the real reason I joined the commune. I didn't think you would want Hattie to know you had hired me to snoop on her but as she now knows you employed me, if this ends up in court, I will almost certainly have to call you as a witness, to explain my presence at the commune."

"Of course, I quite understand."

"I shall need you to confirm why you hired me, if that's all right?" Powell was labouring the point but didn't want any misunderstanding.

"I'm not embarrassed to stand in court and confirm why I hired you," Clara stated firmly. "It's the least I can do."

"Thanks. If you speak with Hattie and learn anything that might help my case, will you please give me a call?" Powell didn't expect Clara to say or do anything that would incriminate her daughter but she seemed genuinely concerned for his situation and he believed she would help if she could.

"I promise I will arrange to meet Harriet as soon as possible. I need a face to face conversation about what's taken place. Once I get to the truth, I'll be in touch."

"Thanks. I don't actually think it's likely Hattie has planted the drugs or weapon. I think it's far more likely she has naively told Scott about me and he has done the rest."

"I hope so. Otherwise, I really have made a mess of raising my daughter."

CHAPTER SIXTEEN

Powell drove to Tintagel in his new Audi, planning to investigate the contents of Scott's study. He might as well add breaking and entry to his other list of crimes. He was looking for the best spot to park on the side of the road, where he could use the step ladder on the back seat to get over the wall, when he spotted Scott in his Land Rover, coming the other way. Scott was in the passenger seat and Tommy was driving.

Although Scott's absence from the house might afford a good opportunity to break into his study, Powell was curious where Scott was headed in the early hours of the morning. Powell would wager a significant sum of money there was some nefarious purpose to Scott's outing. The study would have to wait for another night.

Powell drove a little further, then did a U-turn and started to follow Scott, remaining far enough behind on the deserted road so as not to arouse suspicion. They headed towards Haywards Heath, where the traffic increased, but then went south and Powell wondered if he was going to end up following them all the way to Brighton. When they avoided joining the A23 and instead took the back roads to Ditchling, he was intrigued.

He followed the Land Rover up the steep hill to Ditchling Beacon. He was very familiar with the road and didn't get too close to the car in front. The scenic view from the Beacon attracted large numbers of visitors in the Summer but at the moment, the unlit and sharply twisting road was commanding his full attention.

Powell could no longer see Scott up ahead because of the bends in the road but wasn't worried. He knew that at the top, the road straightened out and he would quickly be able to get back on Scott's trail.

As he hit the summit, Powell could see no lights ahead and immediately glanced to his right. He spotted Scott's car and one other in the small car park. He had to keep driving past so as not to attract attention but went only a short way, before pulling up on the grass verge. He switched off the lights and quickly ran back towards the car park.

As Powell came close to the car park, he could hear voices, muffled by the wind. He crouched low and moved closer, using the cover of the hedgerow, which ran along the front of the road, to stay hidden.

Fortunately, the two cars had been parked close by the hedge, rather than on the other side of the car park. He was able to approach unseen and observe what was happening through holes in the hedge.

He was in time to see Tommy place a suitcase in the boot of the Land Rover. It was the size you are allowed to take on a plane so not huge but large enough to contain a valuable load of drugs or weapons. He wondered how many such bags had already been transferred from one car to the other?

"That's all of it," a man Powell didn't recognise said, walking to the back of his car and shutting the boot. Powell could make out the shape of another man sitting behind the wheel of the car.

Scott carried a briefcase to the man, who then placed it on the backseat of his car. Powell guessed it was payment for whatever was in the suitcase. If it was, then this was obviously not their first transaction as the man wasn't even bothering to check the contents of the briefcase.

"We'll follow you just to make sure you get back okay," the man said.

"Thanks," Scott replied. "We will need more in a month."

"I'm looking at new sources," the man answered. "Shouldn't be a problem."

"Do we need to worry about Powell?" Scott asked.

"I'm not sure why he was given bail but it probably means he has friends in high places. But I don't think we need to worry. He's not going to be running around free for very much longer."

"That's good to hear."

Powell didn't like what he heard. The case wouldn't come to court for months but the man made it sound like he was going to be in jail in the very near future. Or it could be interpreted the man had a more permanent solution in mind to ensure Powell's removal.

Was there a price on Powell's head? This man was obviously part of the drugs trade and such people were notorious for violence. At the very least, this man knew something Powell didn't and that was worrying. Powell realised he was going to have to be extra careful. He could deal with an enemy in hand to hand combat but he couldn't stop a bullet.

Powell headed back to his car and waited for the two cars to exit the car park and start to descend the hill before turning his car around and once again following. He was at the bottom of the hill before he spotted the cars up ahead. He followed at a discrete distance through the village of Ditchling. He knew where they were headed so didn't have to get too close.

On the outskirts of Haywards Heath, the second car left Scott to return to Tintagel alone and headed into the centre of town. Powell decided there was more to be achieved by following the second car. He knew where Scott was headed.

Powell followed for a further five minutes and was shocked when he saw the large blue sign announcing the police station. The car didn't stop out front, where the visitors parked, but headed towards the side of the building, which gave access to where the staff parked.

Powell watched as the driver approached the barrier, leaned out of his window and inserted something into the machine, which caused the barrier to raise. This was not a casual visitor. He had a pass to the police staff car park.

Powell didn't hang around. He had seen enough and already written down the number plate of the car. He needed some sleep and time to think about the next steps. He needed to speak with Brian, who could trace the car registration.

Powell was going to have to tread very carefully. If the occupants of the car were police officers, as seemed likely, and they were dealing in drugs, which also seemed likely, then he was facing far more trouble than he had anticipated at the beginning of the evening.

CHAPTER SEVENTEEN

Powell slept late, having only finally fallen asleep about four thirty. He'd had a large scotch when he returned home and spent some further time digesting what he'd seen.

It was ten when he turned over in his bed and reached for his phone. He was pleased to see it was Brian calling as he wanted to update him on the previous night's events.

"I was going to call you," Powell said, rather sleepily.

"Listen you're in big trouble," Brian replied instantly. "I think you can expect a visit from the police very shortly."

Brian's warning brought Powell alert. "What's happened?"

"The ballistics report on the gun they found in your car has just been finalised. Seems the gun was used to kill a young man by the name of Stuart Brown. His body was found a couple of weeks ago. The police think it was a drug related shooting."

"Shit! After what I discovered last night, I'm not surprised."

"What do you mean? What did you discover last night?"

Powell explained what he'd seen.

"How do you do it?" Brian asked.

"What do you mean?"

"You have a knack for finding trouble."

"I don't go looking for it. It just tends to find me."

"I'll have the number plate checked out and see if I can identify who the police officers might be," Brian offered. "What are you going to do?"

"I haven't much choice. If I'm locked up in a cell for months, I'm never going to be able to prove my innocence. I need to disappear."

"Try and keep out of harm's way. You won't get bail a second time."

"What can you tell me about this Stuart Brown, I'm supposed to have killed?"

"He was a twenty eight year old, out of work reporter. Lived in Lewes and no police record. His body was discovered near Forest Row. He'd been buried in a shallow grave in the woods and was dug up by a couple of enthusiastic Terriers out for their morning walk."

"So why do the police think his death was drug related?"

"They found a significant stash of drugs at his flat. They think he was dealing and it was a turf war."

"That sounds vaguely familiar. Same sort of story someone wants to pin on me. And Forest Row isn't far from Lindfield."

"But why would they kill him?"

"You said he was a reporter. Perhaps he discovered something he shouldn't?"

"Or perhaps he changed jobs and started working for Scott, then became greedy?"

"Maybe. Listen, I better get out of here before the police come calling. I'll be in touch soon."

Powell didn't bother to shower and hurriedly packed a sports bag with a few essentials. He was out of the house and driving away within five minutes of finishing his call with Brian. If the police couldn't find him, he wasn't committing a crime by going on the run as his bail had been unconditional. He didn't officially know about the ballistics report and they couldn't charge someone they couldn't find.

On the one hand, he would have liked to get as far away from Brighton as possible but that wasn't a realistic option. He needed to stay close to Haywards Heath to prove his innocence but evading capture would be difficult. The police would be tracking his electronic fingerprints. Fortunately, he still had the passport in a false name, which he used to get out of Saudi Arabia, a couple of years earlier. It would come in useful if he did have to flee the country.

He decided the best place to stay close and at the same time remain hidden, would be one of the bed and breakfast hotels in Crawley.

Unlike the larger hotels at the airport, they wouldn't require a credit card for identification, when he arrived, and preferred payment in cash.

Powell drove into Brighton and returned the hire car. His neighbours had seen his new Audi and when the police came calling, the nosiest of them would be able to give a description. He didn't want the police tracing the car through cameras, all the way up the motorway to the airport.

In any event, the police would soon be combing all the hire car companies in Brighton, checking if someone called Powell had hired a car. He knew all hire cars contain a tracker so they can always be located. He didn't have a driving license in his false name, only a passport and you couldn't hire a car without a driving license so he would have to rely on public transport.

Powell had switched off his mobile phone at home and removed the battery so it couldn't be traced. As he walked towards the station, he stopped in the shopping centre to purchase a cheap, pay-as-you-go phone, giving a false name and address.

Next, he visited a branch of his bank and took five hundred pounds out in cash, which was the maximum allowed in one day. He hoped it would suffice for about a week of living expenses. The police would trace the withdrawal but the central location of his bank branch would give no immediate clue about which direction he was headed.

Finally, he visited an outdoor clothes shop and purchased two items. He put the black hoody on first and then covered it with a large yellow, waterproof jacket with a hood. It was intended for sailing but its bright colour would suit his purpose. Satisfied with what he was wearing, he walked the five minutes to the station.

His face was obscured from the station cameras until he purchased a ticket from a machine, where he allowed the hood to slip. He bought a ticket to London and looked up to check the time on the large station clock, exposing his face for long enough to ensure, he could be identified when the police came to check the cameras.

He walked to the station toilets and went into a cubicle, where he removed the yellow jacket. He knew there would be no cameras inside the toilets. He exited the cubicle and stood at a basin, in front of the mirror, pretending to wash his hands. He had only to wait five minutes for a young man of the right stature to enter.

Powell quickly struck up a conversation and learned the youngster had just arrived to visit a friend and was headed into town. He was planning to stay for a couple of days. Powell explained, he needed help. He thought he was being followed by a private detective, hired by his wife, to discover if he was having an affair.

The youngster was suspicious at first but gladly accepted the brand new gift and promised to wear it for at least the next hour with the hood up. Powell gave him fifty pounds in cash to cement the deal further. The youngster went off with a large smile and Powell could observe from inside the toilet, as the youngster kept his word and headed in the direction of town wearing the bright yellow jacket.

Powell waited ten minutes in the cubicle before zipping the black hoody to the top and making sure in the mirror, the hood part was indeed covering his face. He exited the toilets behind a couple of other people and walked towards the platforms at a normal pace, with his face looking downwards. His intention was to keep the police looking in the wrong direction. Hopefully, they would think he was still in Brighton.

Powell boarded the Gatwick express train and thirty five minutes later was at the airport. He walked to a desk in the arrivals hall, which helped people arriving to find accommodation. He explained his predicament to the woman behind the desk. He needed somewhere to stay locally but not too expensive. She smiled and handed him a list of cheap hotels.

It took only two calls to find a vacant room. He checked it was okay to pay by cash and that WIFI was available. He received a positive response. Normally, he would have done his hotel research on the internet but his new phone wasn't a smartphone.

He took a taxi to the nearby hotel and paid in advance for two nights, which used up one hundred pounds of his funds. Powell registered using the false name on his passport and a false address.

He stretched out on the bed and gave thought to what he was going to do next. Time was at a premium. He couldn't expect to avoid the police for too long if he was staying in Sussex. As a murder suspect, the police would be coming after him with all their manpower and resources. He needed to get some concrete evidence to clear his name.

CHAPTER EIGHTEEN

Scott met Inspector Doug Williams at their regular spot. It was dark and Scott had once again been summoned by Doug, an occurrence that was recently becoming too frequent. Doug was too used to giving orders.

"So have you found Powell, yet?" Scott asked, wanting to take the initiative.

"No. But that's probably a good thing."

Scott was confused. "I thought the whole point of planting stuff in his car was so he would be arrested and out of harm's way."

"That was before I found out he's better connected than we realised. We definitely don't want him to end up in court telling the world what he knows"

"What do you mean?"

"Fortunately, serving in the police is a very stressful job. It quite often leads to my fellow officers becoming addicted to alcohol and sometimes leads to a dependency on drugs. I have someone very senior in Scotland Yard who is a regular customer for my product. As a result, he lets me know of anything that might potentially put his supply at risk. Someone at the security services, has put in a request to discover the driver of the car, I used the other night, when I dropped off your product. At the moment that request is sitting on my friend's desk."

Scott was worried. He knew if Doug was ever caught, then he would be next in line. Doug would trade information for a lighter sentence. Coppers didn't like spending time in jail. They weren't friends, just business partners, and neither owed loyalty to the other.

"What are you going to do?" Scott asked.

"Don't you mean, what are we going to do. I think we have to assume the request is linked to Powell, given his MI5 connections. Perhaps he followed you the other night when I delivered your product and took down my number plate."

"Do you think he knows you're a police officer?"

"He must do. A check on the number plate by his friends in the security services would reveal the car is one of ours. Fortunately, the car can't easily be traced to me. I borrowed it from the pool and there is no paper trail. However, there is CCTV of the car entering and leaving the car park."

"Maybe it's time to get well away from here," Scott suggested.

"That isn't necessary. I will deal with the CCTV. Then we need to deal with Powell… Permanently!"

"How do we do that? We've no idea how to find him. He may already have left the country. That's what I would do in his place."

"He's communicating with his friends in the security services so I don't think he's skipped the country. He will want to prove his innocence. Otherwise, he faces a very long time in jail. We need to draw him out into the open and silence him before he gets a chance to cause more trouble."

"And how do you propose we do that?"

"I have an idea."

Scott returned to Tintagel, fighting an urge to pack a few clothes and catch a plane to somewhere hot. He had plenty of money stashed away in various accounts and no pressing reason to stay in England. He didn't have the career or family ties of Doug. He'd disappeared before and reincarnated himself as the leader of a commune. He would miss the lifestyle but better that than risk ending up in jail. He would make some backup plans just in case he needed to make a fast getaway.

Powell had found out everything he could about Stuart Brown from the internet, which wasn't a great deal. There were copies of some of the articles he had written but they were all quite mundane, focused on local affairs. His death was briefly covered and there was a photo of him, taken at his graduation.

Powell's thoughts were interrupted by his phone ringing. The only person who had his new number was Brian.

"Hello again," Powell answered.

"So they haven't caught you yet?" Brian joked.

"Do you have news for me or are you just ringing because you're bored?"

"I just got off the phone from Angela Bennett. She received a call from an anxious Clara Buckingham, asking if she knew how to get hold of you. Angela only had your normal mobile number but Clara said it wasn't working and she must get hold of you urgently. So Angela called me to see if I knew how to reach you."

"Did Clara say what she wanted?"

"No. Angela said she sounded pretty desperate. Basically, Clara said it was imperative she spoke with you but didn't tell Angela the detail. I took down Clara's number and told Angela I would ask you to give her a call. I asked Angela not to mention I know how to get hold of you. She assumed you were in some sort of trouble and said to let her know if there is anything she can do to help."

"Give her my thanks and tell her it's all a misunderstanding, which will be sorted out quite soon."

"That's almost word for word what I said. This phone call from Clara could be the police using her to find you, so be careful."

"Give me the number and I'll call her shortly. She said she would call me after speaking with Hattie."

Brian read out the number. "Be careful," he warned again.

Powell had the hotel order him a taxi, which took him to the airport. It was a fifteen minute journey but necessary. He walked into the terminal and found a pay phone near the check-in desks.

"I hear you need to speak with me urgently," he said when Clara answered.

"It's Hattie wants to speak with you. She says she has found out something important and she doesn't know what to do. She's afraid and doesn't know who to trust."

"She should speak to the police."

"That's what I told her but she says she can't. The police are somehow involved. What does she mean? She wouldn't tell me."

"I have no idea," Powell lied. He didn't see any point in adding to Clara's worries. "Give me Hattie's number and I'll call her immediately."

"She said not to call but to send her a text of when and where to meet. She isn't able to speak on the phone while she's at the house."

Powell had forgotten Hattie wasn't supposed to have a phone while at Tintagel. It could be awkward, at the very least, if she was found to be on the phone. "Okay, I'll get in contact with Hattie," Powell confirmed.

"Will you really? Thank you so much. Please let me know what she says."

"I will but if the police ask, you haven't heard from me."

"I quite understand. I will be discrete."

As Powell finished the call, he decided he needed some additional help. He needed both more cash and a car to get about. He couldn't keep using taxis.

He picked up the phone again and called Brian.

"How do you fancy a trip to Gatwick airport?" Powell asked.

"Are you taking me on holiday?"

"Not exactly. I need you to hire a car for me and a few hundred more in cash would be useful."

CHAPTER NINETEEN

Powell had his doubts about meeting Hattie in a layby on a quiet country road, in case it was some form of trap, but equally he couldn't afford to meet somewhere too public, where he might be spotted by the police. Nothing ventured, nothing gained was in his mind as he drove past the layby in his new BMW, hired by Brian at the airport.

Powell could see a car parked and what looked to be just one person sitting behind the wheel. He kept driving for a mile but there were no obvious signs of trouble.

He turned his car around and drove back past the layby one more time, checking there was no imminent danger in the other direction. Finally, having seen nothing to cause concern, he drove to the layby and stopped in front of the saloon car, which he thought was a Japanese make but in the dark, he couldn't be certain. It wasn't a car he recognised.

Powell left his engine running and switched his headlights to full beam. He could see the person in the driver's seat throw up their hands to shield their eyes from the light. Powell was confident it was Hattie and there was no sign of anyone else in the car. The lights also revealed no one was lurking in the shadows on the side of the road, although there was no guarantee people weren't hiding in the trees. He switched the lights back to dipped beam and waited. He had no intention of getting out of the car.

After a minute, Hattie stepped out of the car and peered in his direction, obviously seeking to confirm it was him. He rolled down his window and leaned out his head.

"Come over here, Hattie. It's me," he confirmed.

She smiled and walked towards his car. She opened the passenger door and sat beside Powell.

"Thanks for coming," Hattie said. "I wasn't sure you would want to meet me."

Powell studied her face, looking for hints of betrayal but she smiled broadly and looked him straight in the eye. She was good at acting if this was any form of trap. "I don't blame you for what happened," he said, which wasn't entirely true. He was remaining open minded. "I'm glad you got in contact. I wanted to talk to you."

"I heard they let you out on bail. When's the trial?"

"Not for several months."

"The police interviewed me but I couldn't tell them anything. I had no idea how the drugs came to be in your car."

"Someone planted the drugs and then tipped off the police. Given the trouble I had with Tommy, he'd be my first choice of suspect."

"I guess it could be him," Hattie agreed. "He made no secret of the fact he didn't like you. You were the first person to stand up to him."

"Does Scott keep Tommy on a tight rein? I mean, would Tommy do something like this without Scott knowing?"

"I'm certain Scott wouldn't allow Tommy to plant drugs in your car, if he knew what Tommy was planning. Scott isn't like that."

"Maybe," Powell responded. "He didn't share Hattie's certainty.

"So where are you staying?" Hattie asked.

"I have a house in Hove." No need to mention he had no intention of going back there in the near future. He turned off the engine, feeling more relaxed. "I need to ask you something. Why didn't you say anything to me that day in the car? Your mother had told you why I was at Tintagel."

"I'm not sure. I suppose I was trying to find out if you were a real friend or just doing a job. I hoped you would tell me the truth."

"Did you tell Scott about me?"

"Goodness no, he would have made you leave immediately."

"Who does the car belong to?"

"It's Roger's. He doesn't mind me borrowing it from time to time."

"Do you know a Stuart Brown?" Powell suddenly asked, hoping to catch her off guard.

Hattie seemed unfazed by the question. She thought for a moment before replying, "I don't think so. We had a Stuart at the house for a time but his surname was Green."

It took a second for Powell to make the connection. He took the photo from his pocket and showed it to Hattie. "Was this Stuart Green?"

"Yes. That's Stuart."

"His real name is Brown. He wasn't very inventive with his name change."

"Is he alright?" Hattie asked.

"He was found dead two weeks ago. He'd been shot by a bullet from the gun they found in my BMW."

"My God! That's terrible. Poor Stuart." Then a light dawned on her face. "You surely don't think Scott had something to do with his death?"

"I don't know but I think we can assume whoever put the drugs in my car was also responsible for Stuart's death. How else would they have the gun?"

Powell could see Hattie was churning the information around in her brain. "This doesn't make sense. Why would Scott want to kill Stuart? Someone else must be responsible."

"I don't know why Stuart had to die but he was a journalist and may have threatened to publish something, which Scott didn't want published.

"Stuart was a journalist?"

"Yes and I suspect he was planning to write an expose about Scott."

Again Hattie was thoughtful. "Perhaps Stuart shot himself," she suggested.

"The police believe he was murdered. I'm surprised they haven't been to the house, to interview you."

"Perhaps the police have spoken with Scott. He wouldn't want to worry the rest of us."

"How very considerate of him," Powell replied sarcastically.

"Scott's not a bad man."

Powell was sure Hattie had been genuinely shocked by the news of Stuart's death but she seemed unable or unwilling to link his death to Scott.

"When was Stuart living at the house?" Powell asked.

"He was only there about a month. He left a few weeks ago."

"Not long before he died. Why did he leave?"

"Scott told us Stuart decided he felt too isolated. We weren't entirely surprised. He was always talking about missing the outside world."

"And you didn't know he'd been found dead? It was on the news."

"As you know, we don't really follow what's going on in the rest of the world. That's why we come to Tintagel."

Powell knew it was quite possible for war to be declared and unless Scott shared the fact, no one else at Tintagel would be any the wiser. "Okay, so why did you want to meet me?"

"I was in the basement of the house and I heard Scott talking to Tommy. I heard my name mentioned, which was why I didn't let them know I was there. Tommy was telling Scott, he didn't trust me. He said I was getting too close to you. Tommy then asked Scott if he could deal with me before I became a problem. Scott said that wasn't necessary but to keep an eye on me. He was going to talk to his friends in blue to see if they could do some more checking on you. He didn't want anything to happen to me before I turned twenty one. When Tommy asked why not, Scott told him I was coming into a large inheritance."

"Who are these friends in blue?"

"Well I assume he means someone in the police but I've not met any police friends of Scott's."

"Why haven't you just left Tintagel? Why hang around if you feel you could be in danger?"

"It's not as easy as that. I've already given Scott a lot of money. I never had any intention of giving him my inheritance but based on what Scott said, I'm not in any danger. At least not before my birthday. I know Scott keeps a great deal of cash in his safe. I thought I'd take back what he owes me."

"And how exactly would you do that if it's locked in a safe?"

"I thought you might be able to help me."

When Powell heard the first shot, he instinctively grabbed for Hattie's arm and pulled her body below the level of the windscreen. "Get down," he shouted.

Several further shots broke the silence of the night but whoever was doing the shooting seemed to be a lousy shot as no bullets had entered the car.

Two people emerged from the trees pointing guns in Powell's direction but they didn't immediately fire, which suggested they perhaps weren't intent on killing him. They obviously weren't police officers as they had fired without giving any warning.

Powell turned the ignition key and thrust the car into reverse gear. He was met with the sound of metal grating on the road. They may not have been such bad shots after all. They had decimated the tyres and the wheel rims were scraping on the ground.

Despite the circumstances, Powell remembered Brian telling him to make sure he returned the car in good condition. He didn't want to be stuck with a large bill for repairs. He wasn't going to be happy.

One of the two shooters ran to the passenger side of the car and yanked open the door.

"Stop," he yelled. "Or I'll shoot her."

Hattie was cowering from a gun pointing directly at her head.

Powell turned off the ignition. He was never going to get far in the car and had reached the conclusion whatever their plans, they didn't intend to kill them, at least not right here and now.

Up close, Powell was able to recognise his assailants as Tommy and his sidekick Roger. Powell wondered if Scott was nearby.

"Step out of the car," Tommy ordered.

Powell was pleased to oblige. Within the confines of the car he had no chance to deal with this threat. He stepped out of the car with his hands in the air and took a few steps towards Tommy.

"That's close enough," Tommy warned, pointing his gun at Powell's chest.

Powell regretted having previously demonstrated his fighting skills. He no longer had surprise on his side and Tommy had no intention of letting him get close.

Tommy put his mobile to his ear. "We're ready," he said, never taking his eyes off Powell.

Powell stood still, not wanting to provoke the easily provoked Tommy. Powell had no doubts, Tommy would pull the trigger given half an excuse, even if his boss wanted him alive.

Hattie was standing nearby, looking scared. She had been a little naïve, hearing Scott telling Tommy to keep an eye on her and then obviously being followed to this meeting. She should have been more careful but then that was a tad unfair. She'd never been in MI5 or anything remotely similar.

After a minute, Powell heard a car approaching and the familiar Land Rover pulled alongside the parked cars. Scott was behind the wheel.

"Come over here Hattie," Tommy instructed.

She did as she was told and Tommy turned her around, then tied her hands behind her back with a plastic tie.

"Turn around, Powell and put your hands behind your back. No funny business or I'll kill the girl," Tommy threatened.

Powell was calculating the odds of disarming both men but decided he couldn't risk Hattie getting shot so did as instructed.

"Tie his hands, Roger," Tommy ordered.

Powell offered no resistance and felt the plastic cut into his wrists.

Tommy pulled open the rear door of the Land Rover. "Get in, Hattie," he commanded, waving his gun at her to silence any argument.

Hattie climbed into the car with Tommy holding her arm. Once inside, she shuffled across the rear seat.

"Now your turn, Powell," Tommy said, stepping back out of reach.

As Powell slid onto the back seat, Scott was turned around in the driver's seat pointing a gun at Hattie.

"Let's get something straight," Scott said. "Give us any trouble, even the sniff of trouble and the first person to be shot will be Hattie."

Tommy sat in the passenger seat and aimed his gun at the backseat, allowing Scott to face forwards. Roger joined Powell on the backseat. He poked his gun into Powell's ribs.

Scott glanced in his rear view mirror and then seemingly satisfied with what he saw, he accelerated away.

CHAPTER TWENTY

Powell was uncertain why he had been taken alive. Hattie was a different matter. Scott didn't want to give up on the millions she would inherit on her birthday. Although, how Scott could still expect to get her millions after what she had seen was another question. Perhaps he intended to resort to good old fashioned kidnapping and demand a ransom for her safe return. Her parents were certainly good for a few million.

They had been deposited in the rather dank and damp smelling basement of Tintagel. The room was cold and uninviting. They each still had their hands tied behind their backs with plastic ties but they now also had their ankles tied. They were sitting, propped up with their backs against one of the walls. Powell flexed his muscles to try and loosen the knots but without success.

There was a single light which allowed him to investigate their temporary jail and confirm there was no other way out. The large door at the top of the concrete stairs was the only entrance. The large room was empty except for a single metal chair in one corner.

What the hell was its purpose? Had it been used to ask questions of a previous captive? Had the young reporter been held down here prior to being murdered.

"Perhaps we should shout for help," Hattie suggested.

"These walls are very thick. You'd just be wasting your breath."

"What are they going to do with us?" Hattie asked.

"I'm not sure. The fact they haven't just handed me over to the police means they must need something."

"Such as?"

"Perhaps they want to find out who I have told about their drugs business."

"You sound like my mother. I know we all like to use a little but it's not a business. It's purely recreational use."

"Hattie, trust me, this is a business. The other night I saw someone in the police hand over a very large amount of drugs to Scott."

"Perhaps he was just stocking up a bit."

"This was a suitcase full. I don't know the street value but I guess it would be tens or possibly hundreds of thousands of pounds. That definitely constitutes a business."

"Did you actually see what was in the suitcase?"

"No but they weren't out admiring the view in the middle of the night."

"How do you know they were police you saw giving the drugs to Scott? It doesn't make sense."

"It was definitely two police officers. I followed them back to Haywards Heath police station."

"So why haven't you told someone?"

"I have a friend in the security services. I told him and he's trying to find out who the officers are."

Hattie smiled. "So if your friend knows everything, will he look for you when he doesn't hear from you?"

"Eventually."

"That's good."

Powell didn't want to crush Hattie's hopes but he doubted they could just sit around waiting to be rescued. He tried to give a reassuring smile. "Don't worry. We'll soon be out of here."

"I hope so."

Powell had been wanting the chance to ask Hattie something and now seemed as good a time as any. "Hattie, why did you ever join the commune?"

"Didn't you ask me that before?"

"I think I probably did but we know each other better now. I'm intrigued what you saw in this place."

"I love the freedom. I told you how life at home was always difficult. I was expected to follow a set of social rules about how I should behave. Who I should see and where I should go was dictated by my parents. My mother was trying to get me married to *the right sort of person*. I wasn't remotely interested in marriage. The thought of promising in your early twenties to only have sex with the same one man for the rest of your life is absurd. It reached the point I couldn't breathe."

"Most teenagers face the same problems but don't run away to join a commune."

"I guess that just makes me different."

"There was nothing specific at home you were trying to escape?"

"You mean, did my stepfather abuse me while I was growing up?"

The thought had entered Powell's head. "Did he?"

"No. I don't like him but he never touched me. He was never around enough when I was growing up to even notice I existed. He was too busy making money. He makes a lousy father but he didn't do anything like that."

Powell was relieved. In trying to understand why someone in Hattie's privileged position would join a commune, he had considered the possibility she was escaping something as much as running towards something. "Does anyone ever come down here?" Powell asked, seeking to change the subject.

"Unfortunately, no one ever comes down here."

Powell had a moment of unease. He wasn't sure what caused it but a shadow flickered across his memory and he knew there was something important, he was missing.

"You know what you said earlier about Stuart being shot?" Hattie continued. "Do you really think Scott was responsible?"

"It looks that way. As you can see, none of them are exactly averse to using guns."

"I can't believe Scott would kill anyone. He's always talking about free love and respect for life."

"Charles Manson was probably the same."

"Who is he?" Hattie asked.

"He led a commune in California in the sixties. He and his small band of followers murdered a bunch of people, including an actress. It was big news at the time."

"We aren't going to kill anyone, even if Scott was to want us too, which I'm sure he wouldn't."

"I don't think you know Scott as well as you think you do. Otherwise, you wouldn't be tied up in here, with me."

"Possibly but I know Scott really likes me. He won't hurt me."

"I don't share your confidence. He was pointing a gun at you, threatening to kill you, just a short time ago."

"That doesn't mean he'd actually shoot me."

Hattie was very naïve. Powell was uncertain if she was trying to convince herself Scott wouldn't hurt her, or whether she really believed it to be true. She may be right. Scott might just have been using her as a means of ensuring Powell remained compliant. And there was still the matter of her inheritance.

"What about Tommy?" Powell quizzed. "Could he have killed Stuart?"

Hattie was thoughtful for a second. "Tommy used to be a soldier and has a nasty temper. I think he would be capable of shooting someone."

"I agree. I know he'd shoot me if Scott tells him to. In fact, he might not wait to be told by Scott."

"I'm sure Scott won't let Tommy shoot either of us."

"Well it might be best not to hang around to find out," Powell said, climbing to his feet, using the wall behind his back for support.

The wall was made of stones set unevenly in concrete. Powell worked his way along the wall until he found a rough stone with a sharp edge. He started to rub the ties holding his hands against the edge of the stone. The ties were flush against his skin and as he tried to cut them, the stone was also cutting into his wrist.

He worked quickly, ignoring the pain and after a few minutes the plastic had started to tear. His hands were soon free and he turned his attention to his ankles. He lay on his back and lifting his feet in the air once again used the stone to cut the plastic.

Powell helped Hattie to her feet and was able to loosen the ties enough for her to get her hands free. When he checked her feet he found they hadn't been tied as tightly as his and he was able to simply pull off the ties.

"Now what?" Hattie asked.

"Now you have to trust me," Powell replied. "This may be our one and only chance to escape. We are both going to sit back down and pretend we are still tied up. When they return, I will deal with them and then we get the hell out of here as quickly as possible."

"But there's three of them, only one of you."

"I will have surprise on my side. Now have a quick stretch and then sit back down. I'll make it look like you are still tied up."

CHAPTER TWENTY ONE

Powell didn't have long to wait before he heard the key turning in the door. He was hoping that less than three people would come through the door but it wasn't turning out to be his lucky day.

Tommy led the way, his arm extended with gun in hand and alert to any danger. Seeing Powell and Hattie where they had been left, he relaxed and allowed his arm to drop to his side. Roger followed close behind, weapon also in hand and last through the door was the unarmed Scott.

At the bottom of the steps the three of them approached in a line before stopping a couple of feet away. They looked relaxed and Tommy in particular, had a smile of self-satisfaction.

"We have some questions for you, Powell," Scott said. "Tell us what we want to know and we can put an end to this unpleasantness."

"The only thing unpleasant here is the bad smell since you all entered the room," Powell replied.

His words had the desired effect. Roger reacted first and took a step nearer, aiming a vicious kick at Powell's legs. Powell was faster and as Roger's foot was in mid-air, Powell swept the standing leg away, sending Roger and his gun, crashing to the floor.

Powell was on his feet in an instant, lashing out and connecting with Tommy's knee, causing him to cry out in pain and also drop his weapon, which bounced noisily on the concrete floor.

Scott took a step backwards but Powell was on him with a roundhouse kick that connected with the side of his head and sent him spinning to the floor.

Tommy swung at Powell but as the fist made a wide arc towards Powell's chin, he easily stepped inside the punch, grabbed Tommy's arm and threw him to the floor.

Roger was climbing to his feet so Powell delivered a further kick to his head, which sent him sprawling backwards.

Powell was reaching for Tommy's fallen weapon when he heard the warning.

"Fucking touch that Powell, and I swear I'll shoot you in the back."

He slowly turned around to find Hattie was pointing a gun directly at him. He assumed it was Roger's weapon. Her hands were shaking a little and he assessed it was probably the first time she had pointed a gun at anyone.

Would she actually shoot him? Despite her nervousness, he thought there was a better than fifty per cent chance, she would pull the trigger. There was too much distance between them and her automatic reaction to any movement on his part, might well be to fire. She was aiming at his chest and he didn't like the odds. She was close enough, she wouldn't miss. He stood still.

"Well done Hattie," Scott said, climbing to his feet.

"Everything becomes clear," Powell said. "You never overheard them talking in the basement. There is nowhere in here you could have stayed out of sight."

There had been other pointers, he could now see with great clarity. The Hattie he knew, would have turned the air blue when they were taken prisoner. She would have demanded to know what was going on. Instead, she'd said nothing and he'd thought she was scared but she kept quiet because she knew what was happening and why. It was also why she was so adamant Scott wouldn't harm her.

Tommy had slowly regained his feet. He picked up his weapon and advanced towards Powell. His knee was damaged and he dragged one leg as he walked. "Pretty fancy with those feet of yours aren't you?" He didn't expect or wait for an answer. He held the gun up close against Powell's inner thigh and pulled the trigger.

Powell fell to the floor clutching at his thigh. Blood was seeping out of the wound but the bullet had exited the back of the thigh and it was only a flesh wound. Tommy knew what he was doing. He'd left the bone alone. It wasn't a life threatening wound but it did hurt like hell.

"That will slow him down," Roger said, laughing.

"The only reason you are still alive is because we have some questions for you," Tommy threatened, standing above Powell. "I hope you refuse to answer because I'm going to enjoy making you talk."

"He's already told me most of what we want to know," Hattie interjected.

Powell remembered how willingly he had answered all of Hattie's questions and felt a bloody fool. He was pressing down on his wound trying to stop the flow of blood. His skin felt clammy and his heart was beating rapidly. He knew he was suffering from shock. At home the remedy would have been a stiff scotch but that wasn't an option.

He needed to focus on finding a way out of the current mess. By the time Brian became worried about the lack of contact, Powell doubted he would still be alive, especially if Tommy had any say in the matter.

"Sit him in the chair," Scott instructed.

Roger picked up the single metal chair from the side of the room and placed it close to Powell. Then he and Tommy grabbed Powell under each arm and roughly pulled him into the chair. Tommy took further plastic ties from his pocket and tied Powell's arms and legs to the chair.

"Now, if you're sitting comfortably, we'll begin," Scott said, sarcastically. "Start at the beginning and tell me why you ever wanted to join our commune."

"I'd been struggling getting a girlfriend and I heard you believe in free love so it seemed a good way of getting some action."

Scott smiled. "Glad to see you still have your sense of humour. Tommy, please show Powell this is a serious discussion and he should refrain from any more frivolity."

With an evil grin, Tommy landed a punch on Powell's nose.

"Hit him again," Hattie encouraged.

Tommy followed up by leaning his hand on Powell's thigh. His finger found the entry wound and Powell reacted by screaming at the top of his voice.

Tommy stepped back, shocked by the noisy onslaught.

A few years earlier, Powell had spent one Summer in Japan, studying martial arts, trying to expand his skills beyond Kickboxing and been shown the value of Kiai, beyond the simple grunt when delivering a blow. He was taught that Kiai is more than an explosive voice sound; it represents the projection of sound fused with energy or spirit that blends with the energy or spirit of the opponent, thus having an effect.

Powell had been a bit sceptical at first but kept an open mind and this was the first time since, he'd tried out what he'd been taught. Powell's novice like scream had nothing like the power and impact he'd seen demonstrated by a teacher but it had caused a startled reflex action in Tommy, causing him to step away and providing Powell at least a temporary respite from the pain.

"We'd better gag him," Tommy suggested.

"Then how the fuck is he going to tell us anything," Scott pointed out.

Powell allowed a small smile to cross his lips. Tommy wasn't the brightest spark. Powell's thigh was once again oozing blood and his nose felt like it was broken but he took comfort from having caused at least momentary confusion.

"I'm hungry," Hattie suddenly announced. "And thirsty. I missed dinner, tied up down here. Will this take long? While you lot were no doubt enjoying a drink upstairs in the warm, I was freezing my bum off down here, trying to get information out of Powell."

Scott was thoughtful for a second. "Okay, let's go eat something and you can tell me everything you learned from Powell. Then we can come back here and finish the questions."

"What's for dinner?" Powell asked.

"Think you're a comedian?" Tommy answered. "You won't be laughing come the morning."

The four of them left Powell sat in the dark. He was relieved to have some respite from their questions, even if it was only temporary. He could only hope Brian would be prompted into action by not being able to get hold of him.

Powell also hoped they were all as hungry as Hattie and took a very long time over their food. He wasn't looking forward to them returning and asking more questions. He needed to come up with a reason why they should keep him alive.

CHAPTER TWENTY TWO

Scott led the way to the kitchen and they all made sandwiches and grabbed cold drinks from the fridge. They decided to eat in Scott's study so they wouldn't be disturbed.

"Midnight feast?" the girl asked, as they rounded a corner.

"We missed dinner," Hattie explained.

"Who are you?" Scott asked pleasantly.

"This is the new girl I mentioned earlier," Hattie answered. "Anna meet Scott."

"I've heard a lot about you," Anna said as she extended her hand.

"Don't believe a word of it," Scott joked. "I'm really a very nice person, whatever Hattie's been telling you."

"I'm sure you are," Anna smiled. "Hattie tells me you are our leader so it's good to meet you at last."

"Leader sounds far grander than the reality. Sorry, I've been busy all day. I promise I haven't been avoiding you."

"Perhaps we can spend some time together tomorrow?"

"I'd like that, very much."

"I'm off to bed now," Anna said.

"Where are you sleeping?" Hattie asked.

"I'm not sure yet," Anna answered coyly. "It's difficult being the new girl. Where do you suggest I should sleep?"

"It depends."

"On what?"

"On what sort of a night you want." Hattie had fancied Anna from the first moment they met and knew Scott would also approve. "If you hang around for a bit, I'll finish eating and then come find you. We can probably have a nightcap with Scott and talk further about what sort of night you want."

"Okay, I'll go back to the games room. If I'm not in there, I'll be in the library." Anna turned and walked away. "

"She's gorgeous," Scott said after a few seconds. "A nightcap sounds a great idea. After the day we've had, I could do with some unwinding."

"I think Anna would be up for that."

"Sounds like a plan. She seemed very taken by you. I hope she likes men as much."

"She does," Hattie confirmed. "What I'm not sure about yet is if she likes girls as much."

"I assume you're planning on finding out later?" Scott laughed. "Come on, let's go eat and then we can get back to the cellar and finish with Powell. Then we can have that nightcap with Anna."

Hattie repeated what she had been told by Powell, while they ate their sandwiches. The others listened mostly in silence with just an occasional question for clarification.

"We might have to rethink our plans," Scott said, when Hattie finished speaking. "We may be better off handing him over to our friends in the police."

"Can we afford to do that?" Roger asked. "Surely, he's seen and knows too much."

"Anything he says can be dismissed as wild allegations to try and save his own neck. The drugs and the weapon were found in his car and he's trying to blame someone at the commune but he hasn't a shred of real evidence. He saw a suitcase being handed over but admits he has no idea what was inside. We just deny ever meeting."

"Why can't we just kill him and throw him in the sea?" Roger asked.

"You are joking?" Hattie queried. "I was all in favour of teaching him a lesson for snooping into our business but killing him! That wasn't ever on the agenda."

"You were prepared to shoot him, in the cellar," Roger replied.

"I was stopping him from attacking all of you. That's different to killing him in cold blood."

"The end result is the same," Roger snapped.

"Stop arguing," Scott demanded. "I agree with Hattie."

"And I agree with Roger," Tommy said.

"This isn't a bloody democracy," Scott retorted.

"Why can't we make it look like a suicide?" Tommy asked. "Powell kills himself because of all the trouble he's in."

"And how do you explain the bullet in his leg? People intent on suicide don't tend to shoot themselves in the thigh," Hattie pointed out.

Tommy fell silent.

"We have a tough decision to make," Scott continued. "But I think a dead Powell may cause us more problems than if we let him live."

"How do you work that out?" Tommy asked.

"Because if he's dead or disappears, then his friend in MI5 will almost certainly know we are responsible and will come after us. MI5 aren't like the local coppers. They may not all be James Bond types but we can't afford to have that lot on our backs."

"But if we let him go, then he will tell his friend what's happened and surely that's just as bad?" Tommy asked impatiently.

"We're not letting him go. The police will lock him up and this time he won't get bail. He isn't going to be able to do much from inside a prison."

"And how do we explain the bullet in his leg?" Tommy quizzed.

"We don't have to. Our police friends are going to apprehend Powell in the grounds here. Powell was armed and in a wrestle for the gun, he gets shot. Resisting arrest and trespassing will simply add to his catalogue of crimes."

"But he'll tell his MI5 friends the truth and they still might come after us," Roger said.

"There's a risk attached," Scott agreed. "But we won't be wanted for murder. MI5 are busy in other directions. They will leave it to the police to sort out."

There was silence in the room for a few seconds.

"That might just work," Tommy admitted.

"I'll make the call," Scott stated.

"Am I needed anymore?" Hattie asked.

"No," Scott confirmed. "Keep Anna happy and I'll catch up with you later."

"I bet you will," Hattie grinned.

CHAPTER TWENTY THREE

Hattie hurried out of the office and headed for the nearby library. She needed to relax after what had been a very difficult few days and spending time with Anna seemed the perfect antidote to her stress. There was no sign of Anna in the library so she went straight to the games room. Again, there was no sign of Anna and Hattie felt a pang of disappointment.

"Hattie, I'm glad I found you," Anna announced, walking into the room.

"Anna, I thought you'd gone to bed without waiting for me."

"I was just looking around the house. I was down in the basement and I'm sure I heard someone shouting for help."

"The basement is off limits, Anna."

"But I heard someone. Come with me and I'll show you."

Anna turned and headed out the door without waiting for an answer. Hattie hurried after Anna, determined to stop her from going down to the basement.

"You couldn't have heard anything in the basement," Hattie said, pulling on Anna's arm as she caught up with her.

"I'm telling you, I did," Anna said firmly.

She shook her arm free and kept walking with a determined stride. She took the stairs that went down to the basement, closely followed by Hattie, who was torn between accompanying her and running to find Scott.

Anna stopped at the bottom of the stairs. "The shouts were coming from the door along there." She pointed along the corridor.

"Anna, we're wasting our time. I can assure you there is nobody inside that room. It's just used for storage. Let's go back up and find a bed."

"Not until we look in that room," Anna insisted, folding her arms across her chest and looking as stubborn as any mule.

"I don't have a key," Hattie explained. "The room is kept permanently locked."

"Well let's see if we can hear anything from outside." Anna didn't debate the issue any further but marched towards the door.

When Hattie caught up with Anna, she listened outside the door for a few seconds then said, "I told you. I can't hear anything. This is an old house. There are always strange noises. It could even be a ghost." She managed a small smile.

"Open the door," Anna demanded.

"I can't. I told you, I don't have a key. Now go back upstairs or I'm going to go fetch Scott."

"You are lying. Open the fucking door."

Hattie was shocked by Anna's tone of voice but even more shocked when she realised Anna had a gun in her outstretched hand.

"Anna, what the hell are you doing?"

"I want this door open. I know you have all the keys to the house on that chain attached to your belt."

"I'm not opening any door."

"I should warn you that I have shot a man before. And at this distance I can't really miss."

"Who are you?" Hattie asked.

"Enough talk. Open the door or I will shoot you and take the key from your body, while you are on the floor bleeding to death."

Hattie reluctantly took hold of the bunch of keys and unclipped them from her belt. She found the key to the door, inserted it and unlocked the door.

"Scott will kill you for this," Hattie threatened.

"That will be right after I shoot you," Anna promised. She pushed the gun into Hattie's back before she could say any more. "Lead the way."

Inside the room, Powell looked towards the door when he heard the key turn in the lock. He saw Hattie enter first and it took several seconds to register who followed her into the room.

"Afina, what the hell are you doing here?" Powell asked in shock.

Hattie looked at Afina. "So your name isn't Anna?"

"Get Powell untied and be quick," Afina replied.

Hattie moved to the chair and tried to release the plastic ties holding his wrists to the chair.

"Good to see you, Powell. I had no idea you were in here. I saw all of them coming up from the basement and I thought I would take a look around down here. I thought they might be storing drugs or something"

"But how did you even know about this place? I never told you where I was staying."

"Brian told me what had happened to you and I thought I might be able to be of help and collect some evidence. I joined the commune this morning. Your friend Hattie seemed to take an instant liking to me."

"I'm not sure she likes you anymore and she's definitely not my friend.

"I can't do it. They are too tight," Hattie moaned, struggling with the ties.

"Stand by the wall," Afina ordered.

When Afina decided Hattie had backed far enough out of reach, she approached the chair. "Have you been shot?" she asked concerned, suddenly noticing the blood on Powell's thigh.

"It's okay. Just get me out of here before anyone else turns up."

Afina was desperately pulling at the ties but also found them resisting her efforts.

"I need a knife," Afina screamed in frustration, becoming concerned she wasn't going to be able to get Powell out of the chair.

"Stay calm," Powell advised soothingly. "Take the gun and push it under the tie."

His wrist had been secured palm downwards against the chair arm. He used all his strength to move his hand sideways and managed to create a tiny space between his wrist and the chair. Afina managed to get the gun sight of the weapon into the space and around the plastic tie.

"Pull as hard as you can," Powell encouraged.

They both pulled in unison and Powell swore. The force they were exerting on one side of the tie was causing it to cut into his wrist on the other side.

"Don't stop," Powell urged.

They renewed their efforts and the tie snapped. Powell took the gun from Afina and repeated the effort on his other wrist. The tie broke quickly this time and Powell flexed his free wrists. He bent down and was able to free his feet without too much trouble.

"We need to get out of here," Powell said, standing. "The three stooges could return at any moment." He turned his attention to Hattie. "You're coming with us."

As Hattie came close to them, she bolted for the door. Afina pounced on her, grabbing her by the hair and swinging her around. At the same time she lashed out with her hand and slapped her across the face with all of her strength, sending Hattie crashing to the ground.

"I shall look forward to watching Tommy teach you a lesson," Hattie snarled. Curled up on the ground she looked like a wild animal ready to pounce.

"Get up," Powell snapped. "Give us any more trouble and you won't like the consequences."

Hattie climbed slowly to her feet.

"Give me your belt," Powell instructed Hattie.

Seeing her slow to move, Afina took a step closer and raised her hand as if she was going to strike Hattie again. "Move quicker, bitch."

Hattie removed her belt and handed it to Powell.

"Now give me your t-shirt."

"What?"

"You heard him," Afina said. "Or do you want me to take it off for you?"

Hattie removed her t-shirt and threw it at Powell. She was left standing in just a lacy, white bra.

Powell placed the t-shirt around his wounded leg, then used the belt to tie it firmly in place.

"You'll never get out of here," Hattie warned.

"You're becoming boring," Powell replied.

He took a firm hold of Hattie's upper arm.

"You're hurting me," she moaned.

Powell tightened his grip. "May I remind you, a short time ago you were telling Tommy to hit me again. I suggest you keep very quiet and do exactly as I say."

Powell led Hattie up the steps and out of the basement room. Afina followed close behind.

At the bottom of the stairs leading up from the basement, Powell turned to Afina, "See if it's safe up ahead."

Afina climbed the stairs and disappeared from sight. After a minute, she reappeared at the top of the stairs and beckoned it was safe for Powell to follow.

CHAPTER TWENTY FOUR

Powell was hoping they wouldn't run into any other members of the commune on the way out. Most importantly, they needed to avoid Scott and his bruisers. As they would have to walk past the study to get to the front door, Powell decided a detour was necessary. In his present state, he wasn't confident of being able to handle three fit opponents and Afina's presence had added a whole new dimension to the need to escape. If they were caught, he doubted they would spare her life.

Powell led the way through the kitchen into the utility room and out the back door, which led into the rear gardens. As they took a few steps across the patio, they were suddenly flooded in light.

"Damn," Powell swore, feeling very exposed. He should have realised the house would have security lights with motion sensors. "Quickly," he urged, propelling Hattie towards the woods, approximately one hundred metres away.

He cursed his injured leg, which made every step painful and running at speed out of the question. He was holding on to Hattie not just to ensure she didn't run away but also to support his leg.

He managed an ungainly jog across the grass. Afina ran beside him, nervously glancing behind from time to time. Powell concentrated on getting to the woods rather than worrying about what was going on back at the house.

They made the trees unscathed and with no sounds of alarm coming from the house. He drew a deep breath and realised they were in a difficult position. His original plan had been to simply circle the house and make their escape down the drive and through the main gates, which was no longer viable. If they were to take the far longer circle around the house, keeping to the trees to stay out of the range of the floodlights, it was going to take far longer and increased the chances of detection.

The wall of the grounds was only another hundred metres straight ahead through the trees. He decided it offered the best chance of escape. Any indecision on his part was quickly dissolved by the sight of an animated Scott, followed by Tommy and Roger, emerging onto the patio. Scott was waving his arms around and the three of them were peering out into the darkness, trying to decide where to search first. The patio was again brightly lit but that wasn't helping the three men staring out into the pitch black, beyond the patio.

"Let's go," Powell said simply, pulling hard on Hattie's arm and heading deeper into the trees. He tightened his grip, knowing if she broke free and made a run for it, she would soon be able to disappear in the darkness of the trees.

They were crossing uneven terrain rather than following a path and Powell found himself stumbling a couple of times but continued to hold on tight to Hattie's arm. She was going to be left with some large bruises but he didn't mind her feeling a bit of pain, not after what she had put him through.

The trees gave way to a ten foot strip of grass in front of the huge wall. Powell crouched down and surveyed the scene, forcing Hattie to do the same. He couldn't see how he was going to be able to get across the wall with his injured leg. At least there was no sign of glass or other objects set into the top of the wall.

"You're going first," Powell said to Afina. He finally let go of Hattie's arm. "Sit there and don't move," he ordered, pointing at the ground. He had his gun in his hand to dissuade argument.

"But how are you going to get across?" Afina queried.

"Please Afina, for once just do as I tell you."

He put his hands together to form a small cradle. Afina understood his intention and placed her foot inside Powell's hands. He then lifted her up and she effortlessly pulled herself onto the top of the wall. Her gymnastic training was again proving useful.

"Now what?" Afina asked, sitting on top of the wall.

"Now you get as quickly as possible to a phone and get me some help. Call 999 and request fire, ambulance and police services. Tell them we have a fire at the house and people are trapped in rooms. Once you've made the call, get as far away from here as possible. It's going to take me at least half an hour to get to the gate and I should be able to slip out in the confusion."

Afina looked reluctant to move.

"Stop wasting time," Powell urged. "If I run into trouble, I have a bargaining chip and I'm armed. So stop worrying." Without further ado, he picked up Hattie by the arm and headed off into the darkness.

"I can see why my parents hired you," Hattie said, with barely concealed admiration. "It's such a pity you are going to end up dead."

Powell ignored the comment. He was saving his breath for the exertions ahead. He reckoned Scott would head for the main gate in the expectation of cutting off Powell's escape. He would know the wall was almost impossible for him to get across. There would be no point in the darkness, searching for him in the trees. The area was too big and Scott didn't have enough men.

If they did find him, Powell had the significant edge of now being armed. Scott and his men would be in for a nasty surprise but Powell recognised, if he was to shoot someone, he would have a great deal of explaining to do to the police. It wasn't certain they would believe his version of events.

CHAPTER TWENTY FIVE

Powell made slow progress because he avoided the path around the wall, preferring instead to keep out of sight within the trees. Every so often he stopped and listened for any sounds of pursuit or danger but everything was quiet. Hattie made no attempt to pull her arm free. She seemed to have accepted the situation and was easily keeping up with the pace he was setting.

Finally, Powell was within fifty metres of the gate. He had pulled Hattie down beside him on the ground and he could see a couple of figures moving around in the dark. He hoped Afina was safe and she wouldn't be much longer getting hold of a phone. How she would get one, he wasn't sure but he knew she was resourceful and he trusted her to find a way.

Powell was thinking about Afina and how lucky he was to have her as a friend. Afina had none of the privileges of birth given to Hattie and had survived being trafficked into the country as a sex slave, yet she was willing to put herself in danger to help her friends. Hattie, by comparison, seemed intent on wasting her life. She seemed the epitome of a spoilt child. Perhaps that was the problem. Hattie had always been given anything she wanted. Afina had worked hard for everything.

His thoughts were interrupted by the sound of approaching sirens. He smiled, knowing his confidence in Afina hadn't been misplaced. As the sirens came nearer, he could see the two figures near the gate looking out in the direction from where the vehicles were approaching, no doubt wondering what the hell was going on.

Powell stood up and pulled Hattie to her feet. He would have liked to take her with him but it wasn't possible. That left the tricky problem of what to do with her, now he no longer needed a hostage.

He was going to have to improvise.

"Take off your jeans and be quick," he demanded.

Hattie was slow to react, giving him a questioning look, as if she hadn't heard him properly.

"I said, take off your jeans. If you don't immediately do as I ask, I'm going to have to knock you out with this gun, which is going to leave you with a very sore head."

Hattie removed her jeans and handed them to Powell. She was now left standing in just her underwear and she shivered from the cold. He pulled her to a nearby tree and wrapped the jeans around her waist, tying them behind the tree so she couldn't move.

He reached behind her back and undid her bra. There was no doubt she was extremely attractive but he didn't dwell on the image of her naked breasts. He pulled her hands behind the tree and tied them together with the bra. They weren't the most secure bindings but would hold her in place long enough for him to get away. Finally, he slid her knickers down but looked sideways as he removed them, not really wanting to view her nakedness.

"Sorry about this," he apologised and stuffed the knickers into her mouth. She resisted at first but he pushed his gun into her ribs and she acquiesced. Her eyes burned with hatred and he couldn't resist adding, "I thought you wanted to get naked for me."

Powell turned back towards the gate to see a fire engine come to a stop, quickly followed by shouting from someone leaning out of the engine window, demanding the gate be opened. Powell watched as an ambulance pulled up behind the fire engine, quickly followed by a further fire engine.

Powell could hear Scott telling the men in the fire engine there was no fire but he was told in no uncertain terms to open the gate. They needed to check for themselves that everything was all right at the house.

Scott conceded and opened the gate. The vehicles accelerated through and were soon joined by two police cars. Powell watched as Scott started hurrying back towards the house but the other man remained behind.

Powell had hoped his way would be completely clear but it wasn't. The gate was open but he had to walk down twenty five metres of driveway in full view of the person standing beside the gate, who Powell had decided from his silhouette was probably Roger.

Powell could wait for the fire engines to return, which would afford him some cover to walk towards the gate but that was still risky. Scott and Tommy could return to the gate at any time. The odds were currently one against one and Powell had to believe Roger wouldn't dare shoot him, not having seen the police cars go past. What Roger didn't know was that Powell had no such reservations about shooting him, if he got in the way. Powell was intent on getting through those gates, whatever the consequences.

Powell broke cover and started walking towards the gate at a steady pace, deciding not to attract additional attention by running, especially as he couldn't actually run very fast. He hoped it might take a moment or two for Roger to realise who was headed in his direction but knew it wouldn't take too long. There was no hiding his limp. Powell had his hand down by his side, clutching his gun and was fully intending to shoot his way out if necessary.

Powell noticed the figure emerge from the darkness on the other side of the gate and call out to Roger. Powell immediately accelerated his pace while Roger was distracted. He hadn't been spotted and he could see the two figures engaged in conversation.

Powell's foot was dragging on the driveway gravel and Roger turned in time to see Powell raise his arm. Roger's hand reached under his jacket but before he knew what had happened, Afina had cracked him over the skull with the large piece of wood she had been using as a makeshift walking stick. Roger sank to his knees and fell forward onto the ground. Powell hurried forward, covering Roger with his gun but there was no sign of movement.

"I told you to get as far away from here as possible," Powell reminded Afina.

"I thought you might need my help," Afina answered with a

mischievous smile. "You usually do."

"Help me move Roger," Powell said, grabbing him under the arms.

They pulled him to the side of the driveway and left him in the bushes where he wouldn't be easily spotted, at least not by the returning vehicles.

"We need to get as far away from here, as quickly as possible," Powell suggested. "They still might come looking for us and it's a fair old walk to town."

"It's okay, I have a taxi waiting," Afina answered. "I didn't just call the emergency services. He's waiting down the road."

"I hope he's still there," Powell said, doubtfully.

"He will be. I already gave him a big tip and promised him an even bigger one when we get to Brighton."

Powell was relieved at the thought of not having to walk much further. His leg was aching and needed some treatment.

"You really are amazing," he said, putting his arm around Afina's waist and using her for support as he hobbled towards the waiting taxi. "I don't suppose you've also managed to organise a stiff drink waiting for me in the car?"

"Sorry, you'll have to wait until we get you home."

After a few further steps, Powell turned to Afina and said, "You know, you saved my life back in the basement. That's the second time you've come to my rescue."

"You would have done the same for me. If it wasn't for you, I would be dead."

"But you shouldn't take such risks," Powell cautioned. "I would be devastated if something happened to you. I would ask you to promise not to put yourself at risk for me ever again but I think it's pointless."

"Would you make the same promise?" Afina asked, with a smile, knowing full well if he did make such a promise, it would be a lie.

Powell returned the smile but said nothing. A strange and cruel twist of fate had brought their lives into collision and they had a bond that might be stretched at times but would never be broken.

After a few more steps, Afina asked, "By the way, what did you do with Hattie?"

Powell smiled at the memory. "She's going to be tied up for a while."

CHAPTER TWENTY SIX

Powell carried his jacket down by his side as he approached the taxi, covering the blood stained jeans. He was no longer bleeding but certainly looked a mess with Hattie's t-shirt as a makeshift bandage. Fortunately it was dark and he also suspected the driver would only have eyes for Afina.

Powell slid in the back of the car and informed the driver there was a change of plans. He asked for them to be taken to Three Bridges station, rather than Brighton. He didn't feel it was safe to return to Brighton as it was the first place the police would be looking. He knew trains ran through the night from Three Bridges to London and it would be easier to disappear in the busy capital.

It was fifteen minutes after midnight when the taxi deposited them at Three Bridges station. They only had to wait twenty minutes for the next train to Victoria but it was a cold night and neither of them were dressed appropriately for the weather. The time passed slowly and there was nowhere to escape the cold so they held each other close to keep warm.

Powell wondered why he had resisted the idea of a relationship with Afina, for so long. It certainly wasn't because he didn't find her attractive. She felt so good pressed against his body. In fact, she melted into the contours of his body. She relaxed against him in the way only a lover normally would. There was no shyness on her part. She hugged him close to make him warm as their bodies met but she had no ulterior motive.

He leaned down towards her face and kissed her lightly on the lips. Her green eyes showed surprise but she immediately kissed him back, flicking her tongue between his lips, asking them to open and invite her in for a deeper kiss.

He wanted to smother her with kisses and was about to do so when the train finally pulled into the platform. Fate had once again intervened and the moment was gone. Perhaps it was for the best. He wasn't in the right state of mind to make rational decisions.

The train journey took less than an hour and with the adrenaline having subsided, Powell fell asleep for most of the journey, with his head leaning on Afina's shoulder.

From Victoria station, it was only a five minute walk to the four star hotel Powell had booked while sitting on the platform at Three Bridges. The night porter checked them in, showing no surprise at their lack of bags and the late arrival. Powell again hid his damaged leg. He paid for the room with cash and gave a false name and address.

He reasoned the porter probably suspected he was a married man, who had got lucky with his secretary or similar, and now needed somewhere to consummate their new relationship. It was probably a common occurrence in London hotels.

Safely in their room, Powell immediately raided the mini bar. He had a whisky and Afina the white wine.

"I need to shower and clean this wound," Powell said after quickly downing his drink.

"I'll help," Afina offered.

"Thanks but I can cope. I'll shout if I need you."

Powell closed the bathroom door but didn't lock it just in case he did need Afina's help. He decided a bath was probably a better idea than a shower and turned on the taps. As he undressed, he realised he was going to have to send Afina out to buy him some new trousers in the morning, as his jeans were past saving.

He sank into the warm bath and the stinging jolt of pain from his wound reminded him of its presence. He started by washing everywhere except the bullet wound then concentrated on cleaning the wound. Satisfied he had done the best job possible in the circumstances, he towelled himself dry. He returned to the room with the towel tied around his waist. He took two miniature bottles of brandy from the mini bar and lay down on the bed.

"How are you feeling?" Afina asked.

"Better. Can you get me another one of the hand towels, please."

Afina fetched a towel from the bathroom and handed it to him. He placed it under his damaged thigh and opened the two bottles of brandy. He gulped down the contents of one bottle and then immediately poured the second bottle of brandy over his wound. It felt like someone had put a sizzling, hot poker into his bullet wound and he clenched his fists with all his strength to stop himself from screaming.

"In the morning you can get me a bandage from the chemist at Victoria station," Powell said, once the pain had subsided. "For now, I'll bandage it with this towel. And you need to buy me some trousers and a shirt as well."

"I hope you like bright colours," Afina teased.

"We don't want anything that draws attention to us," Powell replied. "Now we need to get some sleep."

Powell stood up and pulled back the quilt. He had never slept in the same bed as Afina and the idea seemed strange but she would have to be a miracle worker and capable of raising the dead, if she had any amorous intentions. The kiss on the platform had been very much a spur of the moment act and the result of extraordinary circumstances. Why was he always confused about his feelings for Afina?

Afina took off her jeans and top without any shyness and climbed in the bed next to Powell.

"You can hold on to me, if it helps you sleep," Afina offered.

"Thanks but I think I'll stay on my side of the bed as I don't like the idea of anything touching my thigh." He hoped she didn't think him ungrateful. Had his kissing her raised expectations on her part? Was she expecting him to kiss her again? He wasn't sure kissing her had been such a good idea.

"As you wish," Afina answered, reaching to turn off the bed side light. "Good night."

"Good night and thanks again, Afina. When this is all over, let's go on holiday together, somewhere hot and exotic. The Bahamas are lovely at this time of year. We deserve a holiday."

"That would be nice," Afina agreed. She fell asleep with a smile on her face.

CHAPTER TWENTY SEVEN

Powell awoke to an empty bed and had a moment's worry when he realised Afina wasn't in the bathroom. Then he remembered he had asked her to buy him some clothes and a bandage. He glanced at his watch. It was nine thirty so he wasn't surprised Afina was already up and about. Normally at this time, Afina would be overseeing the serving of breakfast back at his bar.

Powell couldn't get dressed so he turned on the television to check the news. He had only been watching ten minutes when Afina returned.

"You're awake," she commented, as she entered the room. "How are you feeling?"

"Hungry and I would die for a coffee."

"I'll bandage your leg, then we can go down to breakfast." She emptied a shopping bag onto the bed. "I hope you like these."

Afina had bought blue Chinos and a check blue shirt. There were also some Calvin Klein underpants and socks.

Afina put a second bag on the bed containing the bandages plus toothbrushes, toothpaste and deodorant.

"This is brilliant," Powell said. "You've thought of everything,"

Afina picked up the bandage and pulled back the quilt revealing his naked body. "Apart from the bullet wound, you look in good shape," she smiled.

Afina had seen him naked before but he still felt slightly awkward. He picked up the new Kalvin Klein pants and pulled them up his legs.

Afina did a good job of bandaging his wound. When she had finished, he brushed his teeth, dressed in his new clothes and was ready for a large breakfast.

Powell filled his plate to the brim with cooked items from the buffet breakfast while Afina settled for some fruit and toast. No wonder she maintained her slim figure.

"That girl Hattie was very pretty," Afina said.

"I guess so."

"Did you and her…?"

Powell stopped eating. "Are you serious? I was trying to help Hattie but she almost got me killed. She was Scott's girl."

"She told me relationships at the house were free and easy."

"They were for some people. She seemed to like you, at least until you stuck a gun in her face."

"Was there another woman for you, in the house?"

"Afina, if you are asking whether I slept with anyone at the house, then the answer is no."

"Then why did you not kiss me again?"

"I was tired and injured. I needed to rest."

"I was surprised when you kissed me. It's been a long time since you last kissed me. It left me feeling…" She searched for the right word. "Confused. It left me confused."

"I'm sorry if I upset you," Powell apologised.

"I was not upset. Just surprised and confused. It made me very happy that you wanted to kiss me but I didn't understand why you didn't kiss me again. I thought maybe it was because of someone you met at the house."

"There was no one at the house. I kissed you because it seemed the right thing to do at the time."

Afina smiled. "I hope I will not have to wait so long again for your next kiss."

Powell suddenly leaned forward and kissed Afina on the cheek. "That wasn't long to wait."

She smiled, picked up her toast and started eating.

Powell devoured his food and they kept to small talk. As they came towards the end of breakfast, he knew he could no longer postpone the difficult conversation. He decided it was best to come straight to the point. "Afina, I want you to take the first available flight back home."

"Isn't it easier to take a train to Brighton rather than fly?"

"You know what I mean."

"Brighton is my home."

"I knew you would be difficult."

"I am not being difficult."

"Afina, you can't go back to Brighton. It isn't safe. Scott or his police friends will find you and either use you as leverage to get to me or will just kill you."

"I can stay with Mara," Afina suggested.

"No you can't. The police records show you were friends and it would be one of the first places they look for you."

"Then I can stay with you."

Powell had to choose his words carefully. "Afina, I need you out of harm's way. If you stay with me, I will be for ever worrying about you. That could get us both killed. I need a clear head."

Afina was thoughtful for a few seconds. "Okay, I will go stay with my mother."

"I'm going to check you get on the plane," Powell warned. "And I will call you at your mother's. I still have her phone number."

"There is one condition."

"What?"

"You call Jenkins and get him to come up here and help."

"I was thinking of doing that anyway," Powell agreed with a big smile. Jenkins had helped him previously deal with terrorists and gangsters. Powell trusted him implicitly and hoped he wouldn't be tied up on some other work. "When we go back up to our room, I'll phone Jenkins and then I'll also book you a flight."

"Please be careful," Afina cautioned. "They will kill you if you give them a second chance."

Powell and Brian met Jenkins at Paddington station. Afina was in mid-air, having caught a 2.50pm flight from Luton airport to

Bucharest. As Jenkins walked through the barrier, Powell was encouraged by the sight of his friend. His leg was going to be a huge hindrance if he was to engage in any fight and the presence of Jenkins at his side would more than compensate.

They headed for a café just a short walk from the station. Powell briefed Jenkins while Brian went up to the counter and ordered the coffees.

"Another fine mess you're in," Jenkins summarised in his strong welsh accent. "I think I may have to move to Brighton just to keep you out of trouble."

"Have you spoken to Hattie's parents?" Brian asked as he re-joined the others.

"I gave her mother a call this morning. I didn't give her all the details but enough so she understood her daughter is a dangerous menace."

"I don't suppose she wanted to hear that?" Jenkins said.

"Not really. I advised her to try and get her daughter away from the commune or she was likely to end up spending a long time in jail."

"That's not going to happen," Brian commented. "Getting her away from the commune, I mean. Hopefully she and all the others can look forward to a long stay in jail."

"I don't want to be in the cell next to Scott," Powell quipped.

"We won't let that happen," Jenkins promised.

"Did you bring the photos?" Powell asked.

Brian took a dozen headshots of police officers from his pocket and handed them to Powell. "From your descriptions, I reckon the two bent coppers are in this pile."

Powell quickly turned over the first couple of pictures then smiled as he stared hard at the next photo. "This is the man I saw handing over the suitcase." He looked at the remaining pictures but none were familiar. "I never had more than a glimpse of the driver and then it was mostly his back. He could be any of these men."

Brian took back the photo and looked on the back. "Inspector Doug Williams. Now we have a name, I'll soon find out who he works with."

"Be discrete," Powell cautioned. "We don't want them going to ground."

"After what's happened, if they have any sense, they're likely to do that anyway," Brian replied.

"Maybe," Powell agreed.

"So what's the plan?" Jenkins asked. "I assume you didn't invite me up here just to sit on my arse drinking coffee all day."

"We need to go on the offensive," Powell replied. "And you'll be pleased to learn, you are leading our attack."

"I always fancied myself as a striker. They get all the glory. What position are you playing?"

"I'm the midfield General."

"I guess I'm on the subs bench," Brian said.

"It's an important role, Brian," Powell replied. "You have to be ready to come on and save us if we get in a mess."

"Talking of messes," Brian said. "I had to smooth things out with the car hire company. The repair bill for the BMW is going to run into thousands."

CHAPTER TWENTY EIGHT

Jenkins' credit card had already proved useful, hiring yet another car and paying for their hotel room. They had moved to a boutique hotel opposite Hyde Park, not planning to spend more than one night in the same hotel. It had been twenty four hours since Jenkins arrived. They had spent the previous night having a few drinks and remembering old times. It was the lull before the expected storm.

The hire car came with a Sat Nav and once they entered the post code of where they were going, it was an easy two hour drive to their destination. They arrived an hour early, having allowed extra time for possible traffic delays. They parked in the car park and knowing they were very early, felt safe stepping out the car and stretching their legs.

"Let's take a walk," Powell suggested. "We can check out the route and get a coffee."

They followed the path downhill and quickly identified the café behind the walled garden.

"Does she meet him inside or out?" Jenkins asked, spotting the patio area with tables.

"Didn't know to ask that," Powell replied. "You best sit outside."

They went inside the café and purchased two takeaway coffees, then returned outside and sat at one of the wooden tables.

"Not too many people about," Jenkins commented.

"I guess this place is quite quiet in the week, when the kids are at school, which is a good thing. The fewer witnesses the better. I've been here a few times at the weekend, when it's been very busy but not for many years." Not since Bella was young. Everywhere he went locally seemed to remind him of his daughter.

"By the way, how is Mara?" Jenkins asked.

"She's good. Afina sees her regularly and I get to see her on special occasions."

"I must take her for a drink while I'm down here. She still in the same line of work?"

"She's still an escort," Powell confirmed. "Seems to be very happy and plans to build a property empire."

"What do you mean?"

"She's just purchased a house and is letting it out to students. I believe she paid a very large deposit with cash."

"I must be in the wrong line of work."

"You don't have feelings for her by any chance?" Powell queried.

"Not the way you mean. I just enjoy her company, as I do Afina."

"Sorry I had to ship Afina off to Romania but she was in danger if she stayed."

"Afina's quite a girl. You and her...?" Jenkins left the question unfinished.

"No. We're just good friends as they say."

"You're mad. Afina loves you and I know you love her. What the hell is stopping you two getting together?"

Powell had wrestled with the question many times, especially since their recent kiss. All the old doubts had resurfaced. He was too old for her and she would inevitably want children, something he couldn't contemplate doing again.

They hadn't spoken about the kiss before she left. They both acted as if it had never happened. Perhaps he was attaching too much importance to a single, brief kiss. They had been cold and tired. The kiss had been a momentary celebration of their escape from danger. Their emotions were running high and they were freezing half to death. It was easily explainable. But if the train hadn't arrived when it did, he would have kissed her more passionately and who knows where that would have led.

One thing was certain, eventually Afina would meet the right man. Someone who could offer her the life she deserved. A life free of danger. What Powell wasn't sure about, was how he would react when that day arrived. It would feel a bit like the first time Bella brought home a boyfriend.

"Let's concentrate on the job in hand," Powell suggested. He had sent Afina away for her safety but also so he had no distractions. "I'd better get back to the car park. I'll call you when Carol arrives."

Back at the car, Powell didn't have to wait long for Carol to arrive and she was easy to recognise. She was driving the very familiar Land Rover. She seemed very relaxed as she stepped out of the car and headed for the path down the hill. She had a large shopping bag over her arm, which Powell assumed contained the package for delivery. She didn't bother looking around for signs of danger. She'd made the same exchange many times before without incident.

Powell pressed the fast dial button on his mobile and Jenkins answered.

"She's on the way," Powell said. "Will be with you in a couple of minutes."

He wished he could be in the café but he wasn't very mobile and couldn't chase after anyone, if it became necessary. There was also the distinct possibility Carol would recognise him before she made the exchange and flip out, warning off the man she was meeting. Powell could only sit in the car and impatiently wait for Carol to return.

CHAPTER TWENTY NINE

Jenkins spotted Carol walking towards the café. She was easy to detect as she was the only single woman in the vicinity. There were no single men sat at any of the tables so he reasoned her contact hadn't yet arrived.

Carol walked past him and once inside the café, Jenkins watched through the window as she ordered a drink, before taking a seat at a small table suitable for only two people. Jenkins nonchalantly followed her inside, walked up to the counter and ordered another coffee and a slice of Carrot cake. Carol was still sitting alone and didn't even glance up from the book she was reading.

Jenkins sat at a table where he could observe everyone entering or leaving the café. He also had a good view of Carol, who seemed oblivious to his presence. He saw her look at the watch on her wrist and was prompted to do the same. It was a couple of minutes before three, which was the time she had informed Powell, the exchange always took place.

Jenkins tensed as a single man entered the café. He was in his late twenties or early thirties and wearing jeans and a black leather jacket. He was tall and athletic looking. Jenkins noted he walked with an air of confidence. With his dark, Mediterranean looks, Jenkins would have guessed he might be Italian.

The man followed the routine of going to the counter and ordering a drink. He then went and sat opposite Carol. He was carrying the same type of supermarket bag as Carol, which he placed on the floor. It was obvious how they planned to execute the exchange.

They exchanged pleasantries like two old friends. Jenkins could hear everything they said as they discussed the weather and the park. They smiled and laughed. The man ate his cake and they drank their coffees. Anyone watching would see nothing suspicious in their behaviour.

After about ten minutes, Carol said goodbye, stood up, picked up the bag brought by the man and headed for the door. Jenkins smiled at the smooth operation and remained seated.

The man took a minute to finish his coffee, then stood up, picked up the bag belonging to Carol and headed for the door. He appeared to be very relaxed.

Jenkins watched the man leave, then was quickly on his feet and followed the man out of the café. Jenkins hung back until the man was outside the walled area of the café. With him momentarily out of sight, Jenkins then hurried to the exit in the wall and wasn't surprised to see the man heading up the hill, towards the car park.

Jenkins was wearing running gear and started jogging. The man heard his approaching footsteps and glanced behind but seemed unconcerned by the sight of someone out for a run. It was a common sight in the park.

Jenkins accelerated his pace and as he drew level, turned and smiled at the man. As the man turned his head slightly in Jenkins direction, he hit him flush on the side of the jaw with a short jab. The man collapsed to the ground and Jenkins grabbed for the bag that now lay by the man's side.

In just seconds, he was once again running up the hill towards Powell. There was hardly anyone about and even if they called the police, the man he'd assaulted wouldn't be reporting a crime. Jenkins didn't bother looking over his shoulder. The man had been too dazed to respond or offer any threat.

Powell was anxiously waiting for Carol to reappear. When he saw her casually walking up the hill, he breathed his first sigh of relief. The greater sigh would follow when he knew Jenkins had been successful. He didn't have long to wait for confirmation as he spotted Jenkins running up the hill, quickly gaining on Carol.

Powell stepped out of his car. He was only ten metres from Carol but she seemed miles away in her thoughts and didn't register his presence.

"Hi Carol," Powell said, walking towards her and waving his hand to catch her attention.

An initially welcoming smile was quickly followed by a look of puzzlement on her face. "What are you doing here?" she asked as he approached.

"I'm afraid I don't have much time for explanations. I need to relieve you of your bag."

A small smile crept across Carol's face. "Scott will blow a fuse."

"True. I think it would be best if you describe my friend here as the one responsible."

Carol looked confused for a second and then realised he was talking about Jenkins, who had joined them. She noticed the bag he was carrying. "Is that what I think it is?"

"It is," Powell confirmed. "Listen, it's important you don't mention seeing me. Otherwise, Scott might wonder how I knew about the exchange. A stranger ran up behind you, grabbed the bag and pushed you to the ground. Feel free to give a description of him."

Jenkins held out his hand for the bag and Carol passed it over. "You may want to rub a bit of dirt on to your clothes, where you rolled on the ground," Jenkins suggested. "Your contact will be back up on his feet shortly and headed this way."

"We need to go," Powell urged. "You can come with us if you want. If you don't want to face Scott, I can get you away from here and help you get started afresh somewhere else."

"And miss seeing the look on Scott's face when I tell him he's been robbed? No thanks."

"You're certain?" Powell had been concerned from the outset not to put Carol in any danger. That was why it was important for Jenkins to take both bags. Carol and her friend from the café would both give the same description of their assailant, which should hopefully stop suspicion from falling on Carol. Scott and the other party would no doubt argue about who was to blame for what occurred. There was no link to Powell.

"I'll see you around," Carol said with a broad smile.

"Be sure of it," Powell agreed. He turned away and hurried to his car, followed quickly by Jenkins.

Powell drove and Jenkins looked inside the two bags. His raised eyebrows told Powell the contents were significant.

"Seems Scott was selling cocaine," Jenkins said, holding up a white bag of powder. "About fifty thousand pounds worth of the stuff, looking at these bundles of cash."

"Sounds like we just caused him a whole load of pain," Powell said, grinning.

"Not just him; he's going to have a very pissed off customer," Jenkins answered. "He has no money and no drugs."

"It's a step in the right direction. We need to keep twisting the screw."

CHAPTER THIRTY

Scott had insisted Doug went with him to the meeting, despite his protests. It was Doug who arranged the original introduction and Scott believed Doug's presence would help ensure his safety. Even the most violent gangster would think twice about killing a cop or someone else in front of a cop.

Doug didn't wish to be seen meeting with a known criminal in a public place but Scott insisted he must show solidarity and attend. They would keep the meeting short. They were partners and had to share the good and bad times. This was a very bad time.

Scott knew the Italian's reputation. Luigi was known for his temper and emotional outbursts. He made no pretence at being a modern day business man. He was a throwback to the old days of gangsters and a violent son of a bitch. There were plenty of stories circulating, which demonstrated his ruthlessness. Most of the stories centred around someone who had upset Luigi, literally ending up in pieces.

For Luigi, it was not just a matter of the financial loss. His son had been assaulted and his property stolen. It was an affront to his dignity and he would be looking for vengeance. Others would hear about what happened and may perceive it to prove Luigi was getting weak. Rivals may try to move in on his business.

Scott was convinced, Luigi would leave a trail of blood and violence in his wake and stop at nothing until he discovered the person responsible for stealing his drugs. He would want to send out a loud message to all and sundry. You don't mess with Luigi Pesce.

Scott had never liked the man but he was able to shift a great deal of drugs and had become Scott's most important customer. Scott was not responsible for what took place in the park. He had been equally left out of pocket but he knew Luigi would have questions and want answers. On the positive side, Luigi had the resources to find the culprit. In doing so he would hopefully also recover Scott's money, although he would no doubt expect a fee for his services.

Luigi had chosen the park to meet. He wanted to see first-hand, the scene of the crime. Scott had given thought to whether Luigi was responsible for stealing his money and whether the meeting was a charade. The man described by Carol could have worked for Luigi. The Italian wasn't a man Scott felt he could trust but for the moment, he had to take things at face value.

Scott, Doug and Tommy walked down the hill to the café. The Italians had arrived early. Luigi and his son, who Scott knew was called Paulo, were sitting at one of the wooden tables outside the café, drinking coffee. Two dark, heavyset types, who wouldn't look out of place in a gangster film, were sat at the next table.

"Scott. Doug. Glad you came," Luigi said, opening his arms in a welcome but not moving from his seat. "Can I get you some coffee? They make a half decent espresso."

"Why wouldn't we come?" Scott asked, irritated.

"I just meant I was glad to see you. You must remember my English is not perfect. What about that coffee?"

"I'll have a Latte," Doug answered.

"Tommy, get us both a Latte," Scott instructed. "Either of you want another?" he asked, looking at Luigi and Paulo.

"Let me get them," Luigi replied.

"That's okay. I can still just about afford to buy some coffees. Do you want another?"

They both declined and Tommy headed inside the café to buy the coffees.

"This is a bad business," Luigi said, as Scott and Doug sat down at the table. "Any ideas who is responsible?"

Doug answered bluntly, "We think someone inside your team must have been talking out of turn."

"We have considered that possibility but the leak is not at our end," Luigi answered firmly. "Only Paulo and myself know the details of where and when the exchange takes place."

"Paulo," Scott said. "Could it have been just a local scumbag who witnessed the exchange? Perhaps a user, who worked out what was happening and saw it as an opportunity to grab a fix."

"This man was not some junky. He was fit and punched with the force of a bull." He touched the side of his face feelingly. "I believe he was waiting for us at the café. *If* he also followed your girl up the hill and took the money then this was a well-planned attack, not a random act."

"I don't like your inference," Scott replied with a raised voice. "It is not a case of *If* our money was taken."

"Okay, I believe you," Luigi said calmly. "I don't think either of you are stupid enough to try such foolishness. This leaves the girl…"

"What do you mean?" Scott asked.

Luigi didn't answer immediately as Tommy arrived with the coffees. Once he was seated at the table with the other Italians, Luigi continued, "We do not believe the leak is at our end. Therefore it must be at your end and the courier is the obvious choice. Unless it was one of you?"

Scott thought about the suggestion for a moment. "She doesn't like me anymore. I suppose it's possible but very unlikely."

"She doesn't like you anymore?" Luigi asked. "Do you mean you used to have a relationship with this girl?"

"For a little time."

"And did you move on to another girl?"

"Yes."

"A rejected woman can make a powerful enemy."

"I'm not sure," Scott said doubtfully. "It was over a year ago when I finished the relationship."

"Perhaps she has been planning her revenge all this time."

"She spends every day at Tintagel. She almost never goes out and she has no phone or other contact with the outside world."

"Do you have a better idea?" Luigi asked.

Scott had to admit he didn't have any ideas. What Luigi said made some sense but equally he might just be trying to divert the blame away from his own organisation. "I don't have a clue who is responsible," Scott replied.

"I don't think Carol was anything to do with this," Paulo added. "She was relaxed like normal. She would have been anxious and shown some nerves if she was involved. I don't believe she will be able to help us."

"It can't hurt to speak with her," Luigi said.

"I will have Tommy speak to her," Scott confirmed.

"If it is a problem for you to question Carol, I am happy to help," Luigi offered.

"Tommy is quite capable of asking Carol the right questions," Scott retorted, becoming irritated again.

"I'm sure Tommy is very capable," Luigi replied. "But perhaps my men have more experience in this area."

"I very much doubt that," Scott stated with conviction. "Tommy used to interrogate terrorist suspects."

"As you wish, Scott. Please let me know the outcome after Tommy has spoken with Carol." Luigi requested. "We need to urgently find and make an example of whoever is responsible."

"We need to get our money and product back," Scott added.

"Speaking of product," Luigi said. "I will be needing new supplies as soon as possible. When can you deliver?"

Scott looked at Doug. "When do you think?"

"I can get you about half your normal order tomorrow," Doug answered. "The rest will take another twenty four hours."

"Good," Luigi responded. "Despite this setback it must be business as usual for our customers."

CHAPTER THIRTY ONE

Powell and Jenkins were parked along the street from the semi-detached house in Burgess Hill, where Inspector Douglas Williams lived. It was early evening and Brian had supplied the address. He had also provided the information, the Inspector's wife of eight years had moved out with their two kids and was living with another police officer a few miles away, on the other side of town. If Doug's life was currently difficult, Powell was intent it was about to get a whole lot tougher.

"No sign of a car," Powell commented. "I guess it's fairly safe to assume the Inspector isn't at home."

"He's probably with Scott," Jenkins said. "Drowning their sorrows and trying to work out who gate-crashed their exchange this afternoon."

"It would be good to look around inside," Powell said. "But it's risky. If the house has only standard locks, it should take less than thirty seconds to get the door open but we'll be in full view of the street. Keep your eyes peeled for nosy neighbours."

"Might as well get on with it," Jenkins encouraged. "No point just sitting talking about it. He could return at any time."

Powell stepped out of the car and together they walked towards the house. It was on an estate of similar houses and Powell guessed they were built in the sixties. The estate had a tired look and most of the houses looked like they would benefit from a coat of paint and some modernisation.

If this was all Williams could afford on his Inspector's salary, then Powell could see why he might be seduced by the idea of making extra money on the side. He was probably fed up of putting his life on the line every day and ending up living no better than someone on benefits.

They walked up the short driveway and Powell already had his set of lock breaking keys in his hand, ready to get to work.

"Wait a second," Jenkins said. He put his full weight against the door and pushed with his shoulder. The door flew open and Jenkins stepped inside. "Sometimes a bit of brute force is better than fancy methods," he explained.

Powell smiled and followed Jenkins into the house. "I knew you'd come in useful one day."

"You hired brawn not brain," Jenkins replied.

Powell pushed the door shut behind them, although the broken lock meant he could only leave it ajar. He was always intending to let the Inspector know he had been visited so didn't mind about the broken door. In fact, it was a bonus. If they found nothing, at least it would crank up the pressure on the Inspector, knowing he was vulnerable in his own home.

"You take the upstairs," Powell suggested. "I'll take a look around down here."

As Powell walked into a large through room, which doubled as the lounge and dining room, he wasn't impressed with the Inspector's choice of furnishings. Everything looked like it had been purchased from charity shops and nothing matched. Perhaps his wife had cleared the place out and these were the hastily bought replacements. A divorce could also explain the Inspector's need for an additional income.

Powell searched the room thoroughly but there was nothing of interest. A desk drawer contained some bank statements but the balance was just a few hundred pounds. Powell took a copy of the statements on his phone.

In his youth, working for MI5, he'd regularly invaded other people's homes illegally, searching for clues to crimes. He realised, the invasion of other people's privacy still came naturally to him, despite the passing of so many years.

As he looked at the statements, he was hit with a sudden thought.

He needed someone who could properly investigate the Inspector's financial affairs. Maybe there were other accounts, possibly offshore, to be discovered. Powell realised he knew just the right person for the job and he would call him later. Hopefully Samurai, as the hacker was known, was still in business and not languishing in some jail.

Powell moved into the kitchen. He searched the cupboards without really knowing what he was looking for. There were all the normal things you found in a kitchen and nothing out of the ordinary. He even stuck his finger in a box of washing powder but though no expert on the subject, was pretty sure it wasn't cleverly disguised cocaine.

Powell checked out the cloakroom but again found nothing so went upstairs to see how Jenkins was getting on.

"Nothing so far," Jenkins announced on seeing Powell.

"Downstairs is clean. Actually that's a misnomer. It's a complete mess but I couldn't find anything of interest."

"He's not exactly living the high life," Jenkins commented.

"I think we should assume he's not stupid. For a divorced copper on an average income, he shouldn't be living the high life. That's the way to attract suspicion and unwanted attention."

"He could at least clean the place up a bit. How can he bring kids back here?"

"Perhaps he doesn't get to see his kids. Anyway, he may be squirrelling his money abroad somewhere. I'm going to ask Samurai to take a look."

"That's a good idea," Jenkins agreed. "Take a look in the bathroom, while I finish off in here."

Powell went to the small bathroom and poked around in the cabinet but was already feeling the whole search was a complete waste of time. He opened the toilet cistern but found only what he expected. He kneeled on the floor, which wasn't easy with his damaged leg, and inspected behind the wash basin pedestal, which was empty.

He was standing back up when the panel on the front of the bath attracted his attention. There was a small gap along the top, which suggested it had recently been removed and not resealed properly. There were four small screws holding the cover in place.

He took his set of lock picking tools from his pocket and used the small screwdriver to undo the screws. He removed the panel and couldn't believe the Aladdin's cave he revealed. There were two plastic bags full of mixed colour pills and a large metal box contained a substantial sum of cash. There was also a gun wrapped in plastic. He wasn't as clever as Powell had given him credit for. Anyone searching the house would quickly discover the Inspector's secret.

"Bingo," Powell shouted out for Jenkins benefit.

Jenkins came hurrying into the bathroom. "What are they?" he asked, looking at the bags of pills on the floor.

"No idea really but I'm guessing they're illegal and valuable."

"They could be ecstasy. There must be at least five hundred pills in each bag. Even at a couple of quid each that's two thousand pounds."

"And there's about a grand in cash in the box," Powell pointed out. "This should make at least a small dent in his finances."

"Let's get out of here," Jenkins encouraged. "Before he returns."

Powell picked up the two bags of pills. "You take the cash."

As they left the house, they kept their heads down and moved quickly but not so fast as to attract attention. They put everything in the boot of the car and said nothing until they were back on the A23.

"We've really stirred up a hornet's nest," Jenkins commented. "Both Scott and the Inspector are going to be feeling the pressure."

"About time they didn't have everything their own way," Powell replied. "Soon as we get back to the hotel, I'm going to give Samurai a call and get him looking into the finances of both men. See if we can't crank up the pressure even further."

"It would be good if he could empty their bank accounts; hit them where it hurts; right in their pockets. I can give him my account details if he needs somewhere to transfer the money."

"I don't think Samurai can actually access bank accounts but he can find out if they exist."

"The amount of cash and drugs we've acquired today, we could go into business," Jenkins joked.

"When we've finished with the drugs we'll wash them down the toilet."

"And the money?"

"Covers our expenses."

CHAPTER THIRTY TWO

Powell had decided they should move hotel. Central London was too far from where they needed to spend most of their time so they booked a twin room at the Gatwick Hilton, once again using Jenkins' credit card. As a large, bustling hotel, frequented mostly by passengers in transit, Powell felt it was a suitable place to stay for a short time.

He was the only person who could prove his innocence and he couldn't achieve anything, hiding away in a small room, somewhere out of the way. There was risk attached but he had no other choice. The police were not going to get to the truth without his help, especially with the corrupt Inspector Williams involved.

On the way to the hotel, they stopped off at a nearby storage facility, where Powell hired a locker and left a sports bag containing the drugs and cash. He had decided against flushing the drugs down the toilet as they might come in useful as a bargaining chip. The money might be needed as evidence and Powell hoped there would be fingerprints and maybe DNA on the money, which would help substantiate his story, when everything eventually came out in the open.

After checking into the hotel, they headed into Crawley, where Powell had Jenkins buy him yet another cheap, pay-as-you-go phone. Then Powell paid a quick visit to a bookshop and purchased a specific copy of Shogun.

Next, they found an internet café and Powell followed the protocol given to him by Samurai, which involved using page numbers and a word count on the page to construct a message. It was an effective form of code as only someone who knew the book they were using, had any chance of cracking the message. Powell kept the message short, asking Samurai to call back on his new mobile number.

As Powell had no idea in which time zone Samurai was currently living, he also had no idea when he would receive the call back. They ordered coffee and agreed to give Samurai an hour. It was mid-morning and by twelve a large part of the world would have had the chance to view his message.

In the event, Powell and Jenkins had barely sat back down with their coffees when the phone rang.

"This is Powell," he answered, confident it could only be one person.

The feminine response came as no great surprise. "It's been a while," Samurai's sister said.

"Hello Tina. How are you keeping?" Powell liked Samurai's sister. She was remarkably normal given her brother's brilliant but rather eccentric ways. She was also attractive and in different circumstances, Powell would enjoy taking her out to dinner.

"We're good. Arrived back in England last month. Peter didn't like the hot climate and the government decided they needed his skills again so all is forgiven."

"Glad to hear he is back in the fold, so to speak. I can't say the same for myself."

"Are you in trouble?"

"You could say that and I need your brother's help."

"Do you want to meet?"

"Are you back in Maidenhead?"

"No. We rented the house out not knowing if and when we would return. We're staying in the Midlands."

"It would be nice to see you but isn't really necessary. If you can give me a safe email, I can send you details of what I need to know."

"Is this phone secure?"

"Brand new an hour ago."

"I will create a new one off Gmail account when I get off the phone. I'll text you the name. You do the same and use it to send me what you need."

"Thanks, Tina. I know your brother is always busy but do you think he will be able to help with this quite quickly?"

"I'll make sure he does. By the way, you didn't tell me what you're supposed to have done."

"The police think I'm a drug dealer and murderer." Powell tried to sound light hearted. "With your brother's help, I'm hoping to convince them otherwise."

There was a moment's silence at the other end of the phone before Tina said, "You don't believe in doing things by half. Once you've cleared your name, I expect you to pay us a visit and say thanks in person."

"I shall do more than that; I'll take you to dinner." Powell liked that Tina never thought to ask whether he was guilty. It was nice she took his innocence for granted.

"My brother doesn't do restaurants so I'm afraid you will be stuck with just my company."

"Much as I enjoy your brother's company, I think that sounds like a very good idea."

CHAPTER THIRTY THREE

Powell was grateful the commune was well organised and had a regular routine. Hattie always went shopping on a Thursday morning and he hoped recent events wouldn't have changed the schedule. Powell and Jenkins had parked their car across the road from the supermarket to avoid attention.

Although Thursday morning was shopping day, the exact timing of the visits had been flexible. They watched impatiently for two hours, hoping they weren't wasting their time, before the Land Rover finally pulled into the supermarket's car park.

"That's them," Powell announced with a feeling of great relief.

Jenkins pulled himself up straighter in his passenger seat. They both watched as Hattie and Roger stepped out of the car and headed into the supermarket.

"That's Roger," Powell said. He's mean enough but less capable than Tommy."

"She looks cute," Jenkins said with a smile.

"So are lions and tigers at a distance."

"How are we going to do this?" Jenkins asked.

"Keep it simple. When they come outside they should have their back turned for a minute while they load their shopping into the car. You come up behind them and ask Roger nicely to go for a ride with us. By that time I will have brought our car alongside and we bundle him in the boot. With surprise on our side, it should be easy enough."

"What do we do with the girl?"

"Nothing. Tell her to get in her car and go home."

"What if she doesn't do as I suggest?"

"I leave it to your discretion."

Powell was relying on Jenkins a great deal. Powell's leg made it difficult for him to move and if Roger was to resist, Powell wasn't confident he could subdue Roger, without shooting him and a dead Roger was of no value. A further death also wouldn't endear him to the police authorities, whatever the provocation.

"There they are," Powell said, spotting Hattie and Roger exiting the supermarket. Roger was pushing a very full shopping trolley.

Jenkins stepped out of the car and ambled in the direction of the supermarket entrance, which would take him right past Roger and Hattie. The sky was overcast and there was a cold wind blowing so everyone was intent on getting in and out of their cars, as quickly as possible.

Jenkins was wearing a black hoody and a woollen fisherman's hat, which was pulled down over his forehead, hiding most of his face. He was staring down at a mobile phone in his left hand to make it difficult for cameras to get a picture of his face. On a sunny day, he would have looked out of place but today he was dressed perfectly for the weather.

When he'd covered half the distance, Powell switched on the car engine. Roger had unlocked the rear of the Land Rover and was starting to put the shopping bags inside. Powell put the car into gear and slowly moved forward.

Jenkins timed his arrival at the Land Rover for when Roger was loading a bag into the car and thus had his back turned. Hattie was already sitting inside the car to escape the cold weather.

Jenkins withdrew a gun from inside his pocket and holding the barrel, brought the gun down hard on the back of Roger's head, before he even knew he was in danger. Roger slumped forwards into the boot and Jenkins grabbed him under the arms before he could fall to the ground.

Powell parked his car across the back of the Land Rover. He jumped out and had the boot open in a second. He grabbed hold of Roger's ankles while Jenkins held his wrists and together they threw him into the boot. It all happened so fast, there was little time for anyone to see anything.

Within less than thirty seconds after Jenkins struck Roger, they were driving away. There was no over revving of the engine or wheel spins, which only looked good in films. Powell didn't want to attract attention and nobody was giving chase.

Powell caught a glimpse in his rear mirror of Hattie standing by the Land Rover, looking bemused. She must have been wondering what the hell had just occurred but they were quickly turning onto the main road and speeding away.

"That went well," Jenkins stated. "Even the bad weather was on our side. I don't think anyone will be of any use to the police as a witness."

"We deserve some luck. It helped Hattie was already sitting in the car; gave you one less thing to worry about. There's no chance of her calling the police so this may never get reported."

"She didn't get much of a look at me," Jenkins said. "But Scott will probably realise it was the same person from the park."

"I think Scott will also work out I'm involved. I'm the only person who would know about the regular shopping trip."

"We've hit them quite hard in the last forty eight hours. He's going to be more cautious in the future."

"That's shutting the door after the horse has bolted syndrome. We've achieved what I wanted."

"When Scott realises you were responsible for today, he's also going to assume you had a hand in events in the park, yesterday. He's going to want to know how you knew about the exchange. That could put Carol in danger."

"I don't think Hattie saw me. It all happened so quickly and she was inside the car."

"You may be right but if she did see you…"

Powell had been thinking about Carol. He regretted allowing her to return to Tintagel, not that he could force her to quit the commune. As long as she didn't admit to ever mentioning her meetings, she was in the clear.

Scott had to at least consider the possibility Hattie or one of the others had let slip the information. It was also possible that Powell had followed Carol from Tintagel. He couldn't be certain Carol was responsible

In any event, Scott would be on his guard and as dangerous as a wounded, wild animal. Whether he knew Powell was involved or not, he might unleash Tommy and point him towards Carol, suspecting she was involved. Powell hoped not as he felt sure Tommy would enjoy having an excuse to hurt Carol.

CHAPTER THIRTY FOUR

It took less than thirty minutes to reach their destination. Powell turned off the A27 at the Shoreham flyover and took the road to Upper Beeding. A large wire fence alongside the road announced their arrival at the old Cement Works. The main manufacturing structures could be seen on the right hand side of the road in various stages of dilapidation. Powell turned left into the half of the works open to visitors, where various small transport businesses were based.

"What is this place?" Jenkins asked.

"It used to be a Cement Works but it's been closed for more than twenty years. I have a friend here who buys up old mobile homes, rebuilds them, and then sells them as good as new."

"Seems like a graveyard for old buses," Jenkins said, noticing the large assortment of old coaches and buses off to one side.

They drove down a road, which split the middles of the site and would once have been used by the staff to get between the different administrative buildings. Powell pulled to a stop in front of one of the many mobile homes, which had been converted into an office.

"My friend's out at the moment," Powell explained. "Checking on an old home near Hastings." Powell had explained he needed somewhere quiet and out of the way for a few hours and his friend had told him to use one of the homes. Powell had explained nothing further but told his friend it would be best if he could not be around for the afternoon.

They stepped out of the car and looked around for signs of life.

"Seems deserted," Jenkins said.

"We'll use that home," Powell said, pointing to a small caravan tucked behind other larger homes and well away from the road. Powell glanced around one final time and then said, "Let's get the boot open and Roger inside the caravan."

Powell took the gun from his pocket and approached the car. He opened the boot and then quickly stepped backwards, pointing his gun at the inside. Roger was fully conscious and looked ready to strike at anyone who came within range.

"Out you get," Powell instructed. "Let me warn you, my leg has been very painful where Tommy shot me. I seem to remember you found that highly amusing. I'm just itching for a chance to demonstrate getting shot in the leg isn't really a laughing matter."

Roger climbed slowly out of the car in silence. He looked around to check his surroundings. "Where are we?"

"It's our turn today to ask the questions," Powell replied. "Let's go."

Powell motioned with his gun to indicate the direction Roger should walk. Jenkins kept a few feet to one side, well out of Powell's line of fire.

The caravan was unlocked. Powell's friend had confirmed all the caravans were left unlocked.

Jenkins moved ahead and opened the door of the caravan, leading the way inside. Powell followed Roger inside.

The caravan was gutted and there were no chairs or furniture. It was just an empty shell.

"Get us a chair from the office," Powell directed Jenkins. "And the tool kit from the car."

Powell noticed Roger's eyes widened a little at the mention of the tool kit. There was a hint of nerves beneath that tough exterior.

Jenkins was gone two minutes and returned with a folding metal chair plus a rucksack.

"Sit down," Powell ordered, after Jenkins placed the chair in the middle of the bare caravan.

Jenkins opened the rucksack and took out some nylon rope. They had stopped at a DIY store first thing in the morning, before heading for the supermarket.

"Hands behind your back," Jenkins instructed Roger, who did as he was told. Jenkins tied Roger's wrists and then further tied him to the chair. He tested the ropes and happy with the results stepped back.

"Roger, I want to tell you what is going to happen next," Powell explained. "I am going to ask you some questions and you will answer them truthfully. I am not one for torturing people. To be honest, I don't like all the blood and gore. However, my friend has no such inhibitions."

Powell allowed his words to sink in as Jenkins moved in front of Roger and tipped out the contents of the rucksack onto the floor. There was a mixture of knives and an electric drill. Jenkins briefly turned on the drill and as it noisily proved it was fully charged, Roger's eyes revealed the first signs of fear.

"Jenkins has done this sort of work before," Powell continued. "He assures me he can keep someone alive and able to answer my questions for many hours, despite the grievous pain he will inflict with the drill." Powell moved closer to Roger. "Did you know that they use a drill like this for operating on people? I would have thought they used some sort of special medical drill but Jenkins says that's not the case." Powell stooped down so he was looking Roger in the eyes. " Jenkins tells me it's particularly effective for bones in general and knees in particular. Although, to be honest, I can't remember if he meant for surgeons mending knees or effective in his particular line of work, which involves drilling into the knee to get answers to questions." Powell stood back up. "I suppose I should be grateful. Tommy shot me in the leg but I'll make a full recovery. If you'd been of a mind to use a drill on me, I would never have walked again."

"It's good for more than just knees," Jenkins interjected. "I usually warm up with simple things like ears, nose, hands and toes. Hey, that rhymes!"

"Poetry," Powell agreed. "Roger, I think it's time to begin. We have plenty of time so why don't you start at the beginning. Tell us how you met Scott and come to be working for him."

Roger hesitated.

"Have you ever listened to the radio show called, Just a Minute?" Powell asked. "One of the key rules is you are not allowed to hesitate when answering. We'll let you off that one but I won't be so generous the next time. Hesitate again and Jenkins will give you a new airway in your nose. So how do you come to be working for Scott?"

"Tommy brought me on board," Roger quickly answered. "I knew him from when we were both in the Paras together."

"How long have you worked for him?"

"About three years."

"Tell me about his drug business. Where does he get his supplies?"

"What's going to happen to me?" Roger asked. "I'm not a fool. You aren't just going to let me go once I've answered your questions."

"I should have explained the full rules of Just a Minute. Not only are you forbidden to hesitate but you are also not allowed to deviate from the subject. I'm not sure Roger is taking us seriously, Jenkins. We need to make him understand that he has only two choices; answer our questions or suffer excruciating pain."

On cue, Jenkins switched on the drill. "Would you like me to remind Roger of the rules?"

Powell was thoughtful for a few seconds as if considering the idea. "No, I guess Roger is asking a fair question. Once you've answered all our questions you will be free to leave."

"Bollocks!"

"You can leave with them if you tell us what we want to know."

"I don't believe you."

"Well I don't think Scott and Tommy will be very happy to see you. They will know I would only let you go free if you answered all my questions. They will have expected me to record your implicating them in a series of serious crimes. I think they might see you as a liability. However, tell me what I want to know and I'll even give you some of Scott's money so you can go away somewhere. You can look on it as severance pay."

There was silence in the caravan. Roger was digesting Powell's offer and considering his options. "Basically I'm fucked," he said succinctly, after a minute. "Soon as you bastards grabbed me, I couldn't go back to Scott."

"That would be my view," Powell agreed, secretly pleased he wasn't going to have to resort to violence. His appetite for violence had diminished. There was a time in his youth when nothing would have been off limits if he needed to extract information. Age had brought a different perspective to life.

CHAPTER THIRTY FIVE

Roger answered all Powell's questions, seeming to understand it was his best and only option. The questioning went on for three hours. Powell would ask the same question in different ways, to verify he was getting the truth. Roger was providing the same answers each time and eventually Powell called a halt, satisfied he had learned everything possible from Roger.

He had recorded the last round of questions on his phone. It wasn't evidence which could ever be used in his defence in a court of law but it might still serve a purpose.

After they finished, Powell put ten thousand pounds cash in Roger's hand. It garnered a quizzical look from Jenkins but it wasn't Powell's money and he wanted Roger out of the picture. Without the money, he may have to stick around. Powell was sticking needles in a voodoo doll of Scott and making Roger disappear was one more pin in the doll.

Unfortunately, Roger was very much the junior partner in the relationship with Scott and Tommy. He wasn't even able to confirm the names of the crooked police officers. The one point of interest was something he had overheard Scott and Tommy discussing, just the previous day. Scott had been stressing the importance of keeping Hattie sweet until her birthday, which sounded like confirmation Scott was primarily interested in Hattie for her inheritance.

Scott had then mentioned a silent partner and said he was getting concerned by recent events. The revelation of a silent partner was hugely important. Powell didn't believe Scott was referring to his police friends. It was the only time Roger had heard mention of a partner.

Roger thought it might be someone in the drugs business. Possibly the very man who Jenkins had stolen from in the park. Roger had been able to clarify he was a local gangster of Italian origin, called Luigi and it was his son in the park. Luigi and his son supplied a host of small dealers in and around Brighton.

Powell doubted it was him because Scott would have referred to him by name. It sounded like Scott was referring to someone who was a secret partner and even Tommy didn't know his name.

Powell considered it likely this partner had some form of financial interest in Scott's business. Either that or he was a public figure, whose identity needed protecting. Perhaps he was someone much more senior in the police? The way Scott had referred to the silent partner as being worried, suggested he was an important partner. Scott seemed concerned that his partner was worried. That was the type of reaction you might have to an investor. Perhaps this partner was helping fund Scott's business and was expecting payback when Hattie inherited her money.

Powell recognised he may be clutching at the proverbial straws. He was so desperate for positive news. He decided he would speak again with Samurai and get him to spread the net of financial investigation, a little wider. There must be a trace somewhere of even a silent partner.

Powell felt there was a possibility Roger would tip off his old friend Tommy that Powell was responsible for their problems. While there was still a possibility they didn't know it was him, he wanted it to remain that way.

Powell pointed out to Roger, before putting him into a taxi, that he was best off not contacting Scott or Tommy. They would not believe Powell let him go without obtaining some important information. There was even a possible scenario where Tommy decided to question Roger. It was evident from the expression on Roger's face that he didn't fancy being questioned by Tommy.

Currently, Scott would assume Roger was still being held captive and that would make it easier for him to put some distance between Tintagel and where ever he was planning to go. Given the connections Scott had to the police, it might be best to go abroad for a time. Powell hinted Spain was much warmer than Britain at this time of year.

Once Roger had departed, Powell and Jenkins wasted no time in also leaving. Roger had some money in his pocket and might decide to place an anonymous call to the police, divulging Powell's whereabouts.

Jenkins drove for a change so that Powell could phone Tina and ask Samurai to widen his search for information.

"Any news?" Powell asked, after brief pleasantries. In theory it would be easier to speak directly with Samurai but he didn't interact well with anyone except his sister.

"My brother would have called you, if he had any important news," Tina stated.

"I know that but I'd still like an update."

"I'll go speak with him and call you back in five minutes."

It was more like ten minutes when Tina called back.

"I have a summary report," Tina said. "But don't get too excited. There is very little concrete information," she quickly warned. "Scott has little money in his personal bank account and no other assets. Williams has a little more money, a savings account with a few thousand and a mortgage on his home. In other words, neither of them have any obvious signs of wealth. However, that doesn't mean they don't have millions offshore in a Swiss bank account."

"What about the commune?" Powell asked, with a touch of impatience.

"I was getting to that," Tina replied. "The commune is run as a Limited company under the name of Lindfield Social Enterprises. There is only one director, an accountant for a large firm in London. Scott is a signatory on the bank account, which basically means he has access to all the funds. The shareholders are both offshore companies based in The Cayman Islands. Peter hasn't yet been able to establish if Scott has any involvement in those companies."

"In a couple of months, Scott is expecting to get his hands on a

Betrayed

large sum of money from a Hattie Buckingham, who lives at the commune. We could be talking several millions. Ask your brother to think about where that money might end up."

"I'll ask him," Tina confirmed.

"What about Tintagel?" Powell had asked Samurai to investigate who owned the property and any connection to Scott.

"Tintagel is owned by a property company," Tina answered.

"I know that."

"Powell, can you please let me finish. The property company is based in Panama and all of the shareholders are other companies based in Panama. My brother believes what he has found could suggest someone is trying to hide the true ownership of Tintagel but equally it could just be a company trying to avoid taxes."

"Is he going to keep investigating?"

"My brother loves solving riddles. He'll get to the bottom of who really owns Tintagel."

"It seems odd both the Commune and Tintagel are owned by offshore based companies."

"It's really not that unusual," Tina explained. "Most companies and individuals with money to spare, will keep it offshore to avoid taxes. It isn't illegal."

"Okay. Can you please let your brother know, I believe Scott has a silent partner. I've no idea in what way they are partners but I'm sure there will be a financial implication and I wouldn't be surprised if they are involved in something illegal. I need to know his name."

"Or *her* name," Tina added.

"Or *her* name," Powell agreed.

CHAPTER THIRTY SIX

Scott placed the call to Luigi, pleased at last to have something to tell the damned Italian. Luigi was running around acting like he was Don Corleone, threatening to kill anyone responsible for his misfortune.

Scott hadn't appreciated the way Luigi handled Carol. He had slapped, punched and kicked her before Scott called a halt. That had set off another ugly confrontation, which was only cooled by Tommy's presence. Luigi didn't like anyone telling him to stop!

Scott didn't believe Carol knew anything of value and even if she was no longer his favourite woman in the house, he wasn't happy watching her getting beaten up. He was also seriously worried Luigi was so angry, he might kill her and that was risky. It could lead to further questions and unwanted attention. It was necessary to keep a level head.

Thanks to Tommy, Scott finally had confirmation who was responsible for Luigi and his own problems. Tommy had returned to the supermarket and explained his car had been pranged the previous day, while parked in their car par. He spoke with the man in charge of security and asked if they could check the CCTV.

The man was reluctant at first but two hundred pounds in cash changed his mind. The security man was shocked when he saw the truth of what happened in the car park but knew if he said anything, he would lose his job.

Tommy caught a brief but clear look of Powell when he stepped out of his car. Scott hadn't been entirely surprised by the revelation it was Powell. After all, he had plenty of reasons for wanting to get back at Scott. They had all underestimated Powell more than once but wouldn't do so again. Luigi could focus his attention on trying to locate and kill Powell and that should keep him out of Scott's hair.

Luigi was motivated not just by the thought of revenge but the belief Powell would still have the money and drugs. Luigi wanted his property back.

With the police also hunting for Powell, it was surely just a matter of time before he was found. Scott would prefer it to be Luigi who found Powell as that would be the cleanest outcome. A talking Powell could still be an issue in a police cell. On the other hand, if it could be proved he was killed by a drug dealer, it would just implicate Powell further in the drug business in general.

Luigi intended to kill Powell, although not before he lived long enough to regret his actions. There could be no reasoning with Luigi. His mind was set. Scott had reason to hate Powell but didn't want to be present when Luigi took his revenge. He would send Tommy in his place.

Williams was almost as much trouble as Luigi. He was running scared and talking about fleeing the country. It must have been Powell, who broke into his house but the answer was to find and kill Powell, not to run away. If the police did capture Powell, Williams was going to have to silence him before the proverbial hit the fan. By that point they would be in the last chance saloon.

Scott's phone rang but the caller's number was withheld, so he answered with a simple, "Hello."

"It's me," was enough introduction. Scott recognised the distinctive voice. "I expected you to call me with an update."

"I was just about to," Scott lied. "I've been talking to Luigi."

"Who the hell is Luigi?"

Scott forgot he'd never shared the name of his customer. "He's my largest customer."

"For that filth you pedal. We have more important matters requiring our focus."

"Luigi can help us solve that problem. Powell stole a large amount of product from Luigi, who needless to say isn't a happy man. Neither am I for that matter as he also stole a great deal of money from me. Anyway, Luigi is what is colloquially referred to as a nasty piece of work. He's ruthless and committed to finding and killing Powell."

"That's all well and good but first you have to find him."

"Luigi is well connected. He's circulating Powell's photo to all the Italians who work in or around the airport."

"You think he's staying around the airport?"

"It's a starting point. Between the police hunt and Luigi, we will find and silence Powell."

"Make sure you do. We've both invested far too much time in this relationship for it to go wrong now when it's so close to fruition."

Scott ended the call wondering why he was always on the receiving end of threats from so called partners. He decided to go find Hattie. It was appropriate that it should fall upon her to relieve his stress.

At least the time spent with her had never been a chore. He had struck the jackpot when he discovered she was not only attractive but sexually uninhibited. He would miss her when it came time to leave but the blow would be cushioned by five million pounds.

She had agreed to give him fifteen million pounds of her inheritance and that would be split two ways. Hattie had actually offered twenty million but he'd declined. He believed his refusal of the larger amount, helped prove he wasn't just after her money.

She thought she was giving him the money as a business loan so he could buy Tintagel but the fifteen million dollars was to be split between Scott and his partner. It wasn't an equal split but then it had not been his idea in the first place. Scott agreed to take a third but would have settled for less.

Once the money was in his Swiss account, he would be on the plane back to Australia. He didn't plan to hang around any longer than was necessary. He suspected it would be a very long time before he thought of returning to the UK. Not that he was going to be committing any criminal offence.

He didn't fully understand the legal jargon but it had something to do with the structure of the companies and the outcome would be that Lindfield Social Enterprises would be declared bankrupt and unable to repay Hattie's loan.

He would finally achieve his lifelong aim of financial independence. He planned to stay out of the spotlight for the next few years. He would buy a boat and sail around the coast, partying with beautiful girls at every stop. Just two months to go to see his dreams realised.

CHAPTER THIRTY SEVEN

Powell and Jenkins decided to eat in their room and discuss what they would do next. Powell was glad to be rid of Roger and what they had learned at the Cement Works was invaluable.

They both ordered a large steak and chips with all the trimmings plus a couple of bottled beers each. They had already drunk the beers in the room's mini bar. While they waited for the food to arrive, they went over the day's events and what should be their next step.

"This Luigi guy might prove useful," Powell said. "Roger described him as a proper gangster. If so, he's going to be putting pressure on Scott to get his money back. He won't accept excuses like it's not Scott's fault."

"Perhaps Luigi will break Scott's legs," Jenkins suggested with a smile. "That's a fun thought."

A light went on in Powell's brain. "He will if we make him think Scott's ripped him off."

Not long after the word went out, Luigi received a call from a contact, claiming a man fitting the description of Powell, had checked into the airport hotel where the informer worked and was sharing a twin room with someone called Jenkins. They were booked in for two nights. The contact was a porter on the night shift, who had carried their bags to the room.

When he mentioned Powell appeared to have a slight limp, Luigi knew the information was solid. He thanked the man for his help and promised him a hefty bonus.

An hour later, Luigi despatched four of his most trusted men to the hotel. He would have liked to go in person but those days were long gone. He had a family and preferred to remain in the background. He was well known to the police but hadn't been in jail since his twenties. He'd been arrested a couple of times but the cases had always been dropped for lack of evidence. It was pointed out to witnesses, it would be unwise and hazardous to their health, to give evidence against Luigi.

The men were under orders to find out what had happened to the missing drugs and money. They were to inflict as much pain as possible on the two men inside the room and once they had the information they needed, they should leave the men dead. It was important it should not be a quick death. They were to have their tongues cut out and their manhood cut off and stuffed in their mouths. It was to be a clear message that you did not steal from Luigi and if you did, you would meet a very violent death.

The men, who were all of Italian descent, knew the room number where the targets were staying. The leader of the men, called the hotel while standing outside the entrance. He asked to be put through to room 316. As soon as the phone was picked up, he disconnected the call. He had the confirmation at least one of the men was in the room.

As the four men entered the hotel foyer, they looked like any other guests, dressed smartly in dark suits. They headed straight for the lifts without attracting any unwanted attention.

On the third floor, they easily found Room 316. It was 7p.m. and they didn't hang about in case other guests should suddenly appear in the corridor. There was no certainty both men would be in the room but given they were on the run from the police, it seemed highly likely they would be holed up in their room as much as possible.

Three of the men stood to the side of the door, out of sight of anyone inside using the spy hole. They were armed with guns and knives for the task ahead. They knew they had to move fast to silence the men inside the room before they could raise the alarm.

The fourth man was in charge and he would be first in to the room. He knocked firmly on the door, prepared to announce himself as the manager of the hotel, needing to speak to Mr. Jenkins about a delicate matter. There was a problem with his credit card. In the event, the story was unnecessary. He had only to wait a few seconds before the door was opened.

When the knock on the door came, Jenkins stood up to open the door. "About time," he said. "I'm starving."

"Let's hope they cooked the steaks properly," Powell replied, also standing. He liked his steak medium rare but airport hotels weren't renowned for their cuisine. His expectations of the kitchen getting it right, weren't high.

He walked to the bathroom and closed the door, leaving it ajar just enough so he could still see into the room. The police were hunting him and it was important to keep hidden as much as possible. His photo could have been circulated to hotel staff.

Jenkins waited until the bathroom door was shut. He was too hungry to bother to check the spy hole. He was also desperate for another beer. It had been a long day.

The Italian burst through the door, the moment it was opened, and was quickly followed into the room by his three fellow assassins. He was surprised it was opened by a middle aged woman but landed a punch on her jaw, which sent her falling back into the room as his friends entered, ready to deal with the other occupants.

"Who was at the door?" a middle aged man asked, emerging from the bathroom, wearing just a white towel around his waist. His face turned to a look of horror when he saw his wife on the floor and the intruders. He bolted for the door of the room but had no chance of escape.

Two of the assassins rushed to the man and grabbed him by the arms. He started to scream but one of the men cut off his airwaves with a large forearm. They dragged him back towards the bed and the man offered no fight when he was made to sit on the bed. One of the Italians stood close beside him with a large knife in his hand. The towel had fallen from his body and he was completely naked. The man covered his genitals with his hands.

"What have you done to my wife?" the man implored, looking at her unmoving body, lying on the floor.

"Keep quiet," the man who had knocked on the door commanded. He already suspected this job was a complete fuck up. They must be in the wrong room. He was going to have words with the idiot who provided the tip. But right now, he had to make some quick decisions.

"We don't have much money," the naked man said.

"I said keep quiet. Otherwise, we'll cut out your tongue."

He was in charge and he could see the three other men looking at him for instructions. They also realised they were in the wrong room. He took out his phone and called Luigi.

"This isn't the right room," he explained. "There's some middle aged couple here. No sign of the people we want. What do you want us to do?"

He listened to Luigi cursing and then ended the call. He knew what was necessary but wanted confirmation from his boss. None of the men had been too concerned about the occupants of the room seeing their faces. They were going to end up dead. This couple were just unlucky to be in the wrong place at the wrong time. They couldn't afford to leave witnesses behind.

He had his back to the man on the bed while he was talking on the phone. He took out his gun, which already had the silencer attached and in a quick motion, he turned and shot the man between the eyes before he had time to know what was about to happen.

He walked over to the wife, who was beginning to stir and shot her in the back of the head. He didn't like killing women or children. In fact, he didn't like killing any civilians unnecessarily but he knew there would be an extra payment forthcoming for clearing up this mess.

He placed his gun in the hand of the dead man so it would have his fingerprints.

"Hold the woman up," he instructed his men.

Then he held the dead husband's finger and pulled the trigger, depositing another bullet in the wife's back. This would leave residue on his hand that proved he'd shot the gun. Finally, he dropped the gun on the bed by the husband as if it had fallen from his hand. Hopefully it would look as if the man shot his wife as she was trying to leave and then shot himself. If luck was really on his side, perhaps the cops would discover she was having an affair.

"Let's get out of here," he said to the other men.

He wasn't looking forward to seeing Luigi. He knew his boss was going to be in a foul mood, which would only be appeased by the deaths of Powell and Jenkins. Next time, he would personally check any lead they were given. When he called the hotel, he should have asked for the men by name not just asked to be transferred to the room. He'd made a mistake but he'd rectified the problem.

For all he knew, Jenkins could be in the very next room and the contact had given the wrong room number. He hoped that wasn't the case but even if it was, there was nothing he could do about it right now. They had to get clear of the hotel.

Jenkins opened the door and stood back to allow space for the girl to push the trolley into the room. She removed the tin covers from the food and identified which steak was medium rare and which was medium.

"Would you like me to open the beer?" she offered.

"I think we can do that," Jenkins replied. The girl was pretty but right now he was more interested in food.

"You can push the trolley outside the door, when you've finished," the girl explained.

She seemed to be hovering and Jenkins realised the reason. "Thanks," he said, taking a couple of quid from his pocket for a tip.

She smiled. "If you need anything like desert or maybe more beers, just give us a call."

"We will," he said, ushering her to the door.

Once she'd left, Powell reappeared. "This looks good," he

commented, picking up his plate. "Good choice of hotel." He sat on the edge of his bed and rested the plate on his lap.

"We haven't tasted it yet but it does look good," Jenkins agreed, sitting on his bed. "I'm not sure we needed to move hotel again but I guess it's best not to take chances."

"We keep moving," Powell confirmed. "I know it was a drag, having to move again, after getting back from the Cement Works but it's better safe than sorry. We stick to one night maximum at each hotel in future. No exceptions. There are dozens of hotels in the area so we won't run out of places to stay."

CHAPTER THIRTY EIGHT

At one in the morning, Powell and Jenkins drove to Tintagel. They had an expandable step ladder, purchased from a DIY store, which remained open late. Powell was worried about being out at a time when the police were extra vigilant, looking for criminals and drunks, so he was careful to stay within the speed limits.

They parked on the side of the road, close to the wall, but away from the main gate. They stuck the note they had written earlier, on the windscreen saying they were broken down and would return to collect the car, the next day. If a police car spotted the parked car, it was almost certain to stop and investigate why the car was parked where it was but hopefully the note would be sufficient to send them on their way.

"It's weird being back here," Powell said, as they set the ladder against the wall. "I'll go first." He climbed the ladder and sat astride the top of the wall like a horse. As he looked towards the trees, the one image he couldn't get out of his mind was of the naked Hattie tied to the tree.

Jenkins climbed the ladder and sat on top of the wall next to Powell. Then he pulled the ladder up behind him, before placing it on the ground, on the other side of the wall.

"After you," Jenkins said.

Powell climbed down the ladder and was quickly joined by Jenkins. They left the ladder in position, in case they needed to make a quick getaway. Not that Powell was doing anything very quickly. His leg prohibited sudden or fast movements.

Powell led the way to the front of the house where the cars were parked off to one side. The Land Rover was in its familiar space. Fortunately, they were far enough away from the main house for the light sensors not to work.

Powell took out his lock breaking keys and quickly had the boot open. He spotted a compartment to the side, which he opened and revealed the tools for changing the wheels. "We can put it in here," he suggested.

Jenkins took the bag of drugs from inside his jacket and placed it in the compartment. They closed the boot and hurried away. The whole job had only taken twenty minutes by the time they were back in their car.

Despite the disturbed night's sleep, they were up at eight and enjoying breakfast in their room while taking turns to shower. Roger had said Luigi ran a small chain of betting shops in Kent. His full name was Luigi Pesce and he was listed as the Director of Roma Racing. Some brief searching on the internet provided the phone number for what was described as the Head Office.

Powell called and asked to speak to Luigi but from the response it was evident he wasn't often seen in the office before the afternoon. He asked if there was any other number where he was more likely to be able to reach him but met a blank. They weren't going to hand out his mobile or home numbers to just anybody.

Powell decided it was worth taking a risk. He went down to the hotel lobby and found a payphone. He called Brian and asked him to find the home and mobile numbers for Luigi Pesce. He said he would call again in an hour. Even if someone was eavesdropping, they didn't have time to trace the call.

One hour later, Powell called again and Brian gave him a number listed to a Luigi Pesce, who had a criminal record and currently owned Roma Racing. He was identified as a person of interest to the police. They again kept the call short to avoid the danger of being traced, with Powell just confirming he was making good progress.

Powell returned to his room and used his mobile to call Luigi.

"Who is this?" a voice answered with a definite Italian accent.

"I'm a friend. I have some information for you."

"And what is your name, friend?"

"That's not important. I know you recently lost something very valuable. I can help you with its recovery."

"And why would you do that?"

"I don't want a financial reward. Let's say the result would be in both our interests. One day maybe you will be able to do me a favour. I have a friend who lives at Tintagel. He tells a story about overhearing someone called Tommy boasting how he and Scott have got one over on the greasy Italian. Forgive me, they are not my words."

"Go on."

"It seems you were set up and have been fooled into believing someone else is responsible for your loss. Tommy and Scott had some short term financial problems and you were the solution. I don't know where the money is but I do know the product is somewhere in the back of their Land Rover. I believe they are about to sell it for a second time."

"It is an interesting story but I am not sure why I should believe you. How do you know they have put the drugs in the car?"

"As I said, I have a friend at the house."

"It would be foolish of you to lie to me," Luigi warned.

"It's easy enough to check out. Pay Scott a visit and see if my information is correct. What have you to lose?"

"How can I contact you?" Luigi asked.

"You can't."

"But if I find something of interest in the Land Rover, I will want to thank you properly."

"I'll be in touch again. You'll be needing a new supplier, I guess?"

"Now I understand. You want to take over Scott's business. I like entrepreneurs. Give me a call in a few days and we can talk further. Of course, that is contingent on your information being correct."

"It is," Powell said and ended the call.

CHAPTER THIRTY NINE

When Powell finished the call with Luigi, he was in a good mood. He was quietly confident Luigi had taken the bait and there was trouble in store for Scott.

"I think that went quite well," Powell summarised, as he turned to see Jenkins glued to the television screen. Receiving no response and seeing the worried look on the face of Jenkins, he asked, "What's happened?"

Jenkins didn't answer for a few seconds and Powell looked at the television to see what had captured Jenkins' attention. Almost immediately the news item changed so he was none the wiser.

Jenkins turned to Powell. "Two people were found dead yesterday evening, in the same hotel where we checked out yesterday afternoon," Jenkins explained.

"It could be a coincidence," Powell suggested but his good mood was fast evaporating. He wasn't much of a believer in coincidences.

"It could be but what if they were after us and those poor people got in the way?"

"How did they die?" Powell queried. "Did the news say they were murdered?"

"Not exactly. They were unexplained deaths."

"That could mean suicides. It's just as well we moved out. Even if it was nothing to do with us, the police would have wanted to interview all the guests. Looks like we had a narrow escape."

"Probably not entirely true. The police will likely check who stayed in the room the previous night. That will eventually lead them to me.

"You gave your home address in Wales so they won't find anyone at home. I doubt they will track you down before this is all resolved.

"I'll have to be careful how I use my credit cards. They are easily tracked, as is my phone."

"If necessary, we can use some of the cash we've inherited to pay the bills.

"You should talk to Brian," Jenkins suggested. "See what he can find out about how the couple died."

"I will. One day it would be nice though to be able to call him and not have to ask for a favour."

"That's the only type of call I ever get from you," Jenkins said with a mock, pained expression.

"True but I know you're bored and sitting by the phone, waiting for me to call."

"Well life certainly hasn't been dull since we met.

"I even took you on holiday with me to the sun."

"If you mean bloody Saudi Arabia that isn't funny."

"It was a bit hairy," Powell acknowledged.

"So the call with Luigi went well?" Jenkins enquired.

"He thinks I'm trying to muscle in on Scott's business and will check the Land Rover."

"Wish I could be there."

"Me too. I'll go call Brian. You get ready for us to check out. I've chosen a hotel in Reigate to stay tonight."

Powell once again visited the payphones in the foyer. He checked nobody was paying undue attention to the phones, in case his earlier calls had been traced, although it seemed extremely unlikely as he had kept the calls short. But he wasn't abreast of modern technology and didn't know if the authorities could now trace calls in seconds rather than minutes. It wasn't something they would announce to the world.

Satisfied he could detect nothing out of the ordinary, he put in a call to Brian, who promised to investigate and get back to Powell as soon as he had obtained a copy of the police reports. Powell didn't say why he wanted to know about the two deaths but stressed he needed to know the room number where the people were staying. Brian realised it wasn't wise to ask the reason behind the questions, over the phone. Powell hoped their deaths were not linked to him in any way. His conscience was already full to bursting with regrets.

Powell was about to return to the room when his mobile rang. He was hopeful the impromptu call signalled Samurai had finally discovered something useful. Tina was still the only person who had his number.

"Hi Tina," he answered, walking towards a quiet area of the foyer. "I hope you're calling with some good news."

"Hi Powell. I'm not sure. Peter has stumbled across something strange, he thinks you should know about."

"Tell me," he said in a calm voice, which disguised the sudden surge of excitement he was feeling.

"As you requested, he's been trying to discover the name of the person who really owns Tintagel. There are various accountants and lawyers involved with the myriad of companies but he's finally found a tenuous paper trail link to someone who's name has cropped up as a signatory on a loan document. It doesn't mean this person owns Tintagel and it could just be a coincidence but …"

"Tina, who is it?" Powell urged. This was turning out to be a day of coincidences.

CHAPTER FORTY

Powell arrived at the house in Putney and as the maid showed him through to the lounge, he couldn't help but remember his first visit only a couple of weeks earlier, since when his life had been in turmoil. On that occasion, he had been invited by Clara Buckingham and thought it strange her husband didn't seem to really want to be at the meeting. This time, the meeting was with Charles Buckingham and he was about to receive the shock of his life.

Charles entered the room and Powell went through the routine of shaking hands despite how he felt about the man.

"What was it you wanted to see me about?" Charles asked, grumpily. "I'm a very busy man."

"I'm sure you are," Powell replied, sitting on the sofa. "All those companies you are involved with must keep you extremely busy."

"Companies? What companies?"

"The ones in Panama you've used to disguise your holdings in certain UK companies."

"What the hell are you talking about," Charles demanded. "What's all this nonsense about Panama?"

"I've been trying to establish who owned Tintagel and you can imagine my surprise when I discovered it was you."

"I have no idea what you are talking about," Charles replied, in a raised voice. "This really is a waste of my time."

"I want to come to some sort of arrangement with you. Thanks to you and Scott, I need to get out of the country. I need some money to make that possible. I have assets. I own a house and a bar but I don't have much cash."

"So you came here to try and extort money from me?"

"I think blackmail would be a better description. You pay me a million pounds and I'll forget what I know about your business dealings."

"You're bluffing. You don't know anything. I've done nothing wrong."

"I'm not wearing a wire," Powell said, opening his jacket. "Search me. Then we can stop all this bullshit and get down to talking numbers."

"I'm going to call the police," Charles threatened.

"If you were going to call the police, you would have already done so. In fact, an innocent person would have had the police waiting for me when I arrived. You couldn't risk calling the police until you found out what I knew and whether I was a threat to your plans. As I said before, I need to get out of the country. It's in your interest to help me get as far away as possible."

Charles Buckingham was thoughtful for a second. Then he walked towards Powell and patted down his body. He checked the contents of his pockets and seemingly satisfied, stepped backwards.

"It was most unfortunate for both of us, my wife insisted on hiring your services."

"I have no ties to this country," Powell said. "I would enjoy a clean break and fresh start somewhere with a warm climate. I am even willing to sell you my bar in exchange for a fair price. I just need a quick deal and the money up front so I can skip the country."

"How will you do that?"

"Well I'm not likely to tell you so you can arrange for the police to arrest me. I can get out of the country. I have access to a passport in a different name. But I don't intend to leave without sufficient funds to have a decent lifestyle."

"I repeat, I haven't done anything illegal."

"I'm not sure about that. Conspiracy charges can cover a great number of circumstances, including murder."

"Murder? What do you take me for? I haven't been involved with any murders."

"Possibly not but I'm sure you don't want your personal life all over the front pages of the newspapers. It would make especially interesting reading for your wife and stepdaughter."

Charles walked to a globe standing on one side of the room. When he opened the top it revealed a small bar with a collection of alcohol and glasses. "Do you want one?" he asked.

"I'll have a malt whisky, if you have one?"

Charles poured two glasses of malt Scotch and handed one to Powell. "Tell me something to make me believe you aren't just bluffing," Charles requested.

"CCH Holdings. Does the CCH stand for Charles, Clara and Hattie by any chance?"

"Yes it does. You really have done your homework."

"I had some expert help."

"So you aren't the only one who knows about my business dealings?" Charles asked, suddenly concerned.

"Don't worry. My help was a hacker who works outside the law. He will only publicise what he knows if something unfortunate should happen to me."

"If you know my business dealings as well as you say you do, then you know I'm not exactly flush with money."

"I'm not an unreasonable man. I need some immediate cash but I'm willing to wait for the balance until Hattie hands over her inheritance to Scott."

"I begin to wish you had been my partner not Scott," Charles said. "I can give you fifty thousand in cash tomorrow," he offered.

"That would be acceptable for the time being. I expect the other money within one month of Hattie's birthday."

"Agreed."

"Tell me," Powell asked. "How did you ever meet Scott? He doesn't seem like the type of person you would normally associate with."

"I was desperate. My businesses were leaking money and I had Tintagel available to rent at half the going rate. He said he was interested and the rest, as they say, is history."

"Did Clara not realise you owned Tintagel?"

"To be honest, she hasn't a clue about my business dealings. She has her own money."

"Who had the idea about Hattie's inheritance?"

"It was mine. Her grandfather never should have left her so much money in the first place. She's a spoilt child. She would just squander the money."

"She might not have fallen for Scott or agreed to make the donation."

"She's predictable. The more I told her, I didn't want her to see him or be at the commune, the more certain it was she would do what we wanted."

"You could have told her the truth and asked her to invest in your business."

"We aren't close enough and that would have involved telling her mother. It wasn't a serious option."

"Just out of interest, where did all your money go?"

"A couple of bad investments. Since the stock market collapsed, I've been struggling. Robbing Peter to pay Paul. The interest alone on my loans is crippling me and without Hattie's money, I will be bankrupt by the end of the year."

"You said your wife has money? Couldn't she have helped?"

"Possibly but I didn't want to ask her? It would have meant the end of our marriage if I told her I'd lost everything."

So much for the wedding vow about for richer, for poorer! Powell was amused and shocked by Charles' logic. He couldn't face asking his wife for money but it was okay to steal from his stepdaughter. His moral compass was really in a mess.

"I want you to tell Scott and his pit bull Tommy to leave me alone. If they don't and anything happens to me, my friends will publish the truth about your financial situation and the walls of this beautiful home will come tumbling down real quick."

"I'll tell Scott to leave you alone," Charles confirmed. "I don't know anyone called Tommy."

There was a sudden commotion at the door to the room. Hattie burst in, followed by Clara, who seemed to be unsuccessfully trying to hold her back.

"You fucking bastard," Hattie shouted at her stepfather. "How could you betray your own daughter like that!"

Charles was shocked by the sudden appearance of Hattie and Clara.

Hattie was rushing at her stepfather, screaming obscenities. She had shaken loose of her mother.

Powell felt no urgency to intervene. After what he'd gone through, watching Hattie trying to claw at her stepfather's face, while he fought her off, was not the worst entertainment. Charles had his arms in front of his face, trying to avoid Hattie's blows. Hattie's mother was desperately trying to pull her daughter away from her stepfather.

Powell did feel sorry for Clara, she was the innocent victim of her husband's scheming. She had been horribly betrayed by her husband. His actions had destroyed her family.

They had been listening to everything said in the lounge from a bedroom upstairs. Clara had agreed the previous day to the planting of the listening device in the lounge. Powell had been nonspecific about what she would hear but insisted she and Hattie should listen in on the meeting as they would learn something of vital importance. Clara had been doubtful but agreed as she felt she owed Powell something. How Clara had managed to get Hattie to visit, he had no idea but she had obviously succeeded.

Powell leisurely stood up and grabbed Hattie by the collar and without letting go, dragged her away and forced her to sit on the sofa.

"That's enough, Hattie," Powell demanded, as she continued to struggle. She finally stopped and he let go of her collar.

"How could you stoop so low?" Clara asked her husband. "I can live with you lying to me but Hattie's your daughter." She flopped into one of the armchairs, obviously in shock. "I want you to leave," she said firmly to Charles. "You disgust me. I want you to leave now."

Charles seemed happy to leave. He hurried towards the door.

"Actually she's not my daughter. I'll stay at the club," he muttered, as he passed Clara.

"And don't fucking come back," Hattie shouted, as he went out the door.

Quiet descended on the room for a moment as both Clara and Hattie were lost in their thoughts.

"What happens next?" Clara asked after a minute, visibly in shock.

CHAPTER FORTY ONE

Powell, Clara and Hattie's unexpected arrival at Haywards Heath police station, accompanied by a very expensive solicitor, provided by Clara Buckingham, had caused considerable consternation. It took some time for the man behind the desk to understand, their most sought after suspect was asking to speak with whoever was in charge of his case.

The solicitor was primarily present for the benefit of Hattie but she was determined to tell the police everything she knew about Scott and his involvement in drugs and violence. She was intent on seeing Scott go to prison for as long as possible and didn't seem too bothered about the consequences of her revelations. It was up to her solicitor to make sure she didn't incriminate herself and also end up behind bars.

Hattie seemed like a changed person in just a few short hours. Her ideal of the commune had been rent asunder as she realised how Scott and her stepfather had conspired to steal her inheritance.

She had also come to realise that the guns at the house weren't just for protection. Someone at the house had almost certainly been responsible for Stuart's death.

It was like all the rebellion and fight had drained away, leaving just the young girl behind. She had said sorry to Powell and he had been conciliatory. He recognised that while Hattie was fully cooperating with the police, she was in effect helping to clear his name.

After several hours of interrogation, Powell recognised a change in the attitudes of the detectives. They were coming around to the opinion, he was an innocent man. There were to be no new charges. Officially, he was still on bail for the drugs charges but it would be only a matter of time before the Crown Prosecution service dropped those charges.

Clara was interviewed and confirmed her reasons for hiring Powell. She was also able to describe how she met Hattie in the café and told her about Powell. Hattie then confirmed she told Scott about Powell. She couldn't be sure Scott had acted on the information but what she did know for certain, was that Tommy had told her to take Powell shopping and she wasn't to use the Land Rover. The implication for finding the drugs and gun in Powell's car was circumstantial but pointed further suspicion at Tommy.

Tommy was arrested for kidnapping and shooting Powell in the leg. Hattie had been a witness and the police had found the weapon he used, when they raided Tintagel. Hattie and Powell's evidence combined was enough for the police to get search warrants and they had run a forensic toothcomb over Tintagel. They had found drugs in the basement as well as blood spots matching Powell's blood.

Hattie gave a detailed statement about Scott's drug dealing. The police had promised her immunity from prosecution for any charges pertaining to drugs in return for her cooperation but if she was found to be involved in the murder of Stuart Brown, that would be a different matter.

They corroborated her story by interviewing Carol, who was also given a promise of no prosecution in return for her testimony. She was happy to confirm the details of the exchanges, although she stuck by the story that she didn't know what was inside the bags. She refused to explain the bruises on her face and press any charges against Luigi. She knew his reputation.

The police were excited to have at least the beginnings of a case against Luigi Pesce's son, if not the father. DNA and fingerprint tests of the shopping bags containing the drugs and money were carried out and prints on both bags matched those of Luigi's son. The slippery Luigi couldn't be charged but his son was definitely going to jail.

When Scott was arrested, he was found to be in good health so Luigi hadn't yet paid him a visit and discovered the drugs in the rear of the Land Rover. Either that or Scott had convinced him they weren't the same drugs, which had always been a possibility.

Powell realised he had to add Luigi to the long list of people who would be happy to see him dead. Luigi was a little different to most because he lived locally. Powell hoped Luigi would keep away now the police were more focused than usual on his activities. He could no longer recover any drugs or money from Powell. It was in his own self-interest to leave well alone but it wouldn't stop Powell being extra cautious.

Hattie didn't know for certain who had killed Stuart Brown, though she suspected it was Tommy. She didn't believe Scott was capable of having pulled the trigger but he could have given the order. A view that was supported by Powell, without any actual proof.

Unfortunately, there was no evidence linking anyone to the gun found in Powel's car. Tommy had used a different weapon when he shot Powell so he either owned two guns or the one that killed Stuart Brown, belonged to someone else. Any DNA evidence linking Stuart Brown to the house or anyone living at the house was irrelevant, given it wasn't in dispute he had been living at Tintagel for several months. The murder investigation would be ongoing

What upset Hattie most was the fact, in the eyes of the law, her stepfather had committed no crime. Being a terrible father and betraying your stepdaughter's trust, was not a crime. The business dealings were legitimate, if a little shady but nothing linked him to Scott's various crimes. The police intended to investigate him further in case they could get him on a conspiracy charge but they hadn't been confident about their chances.

Powell heard that Scott's two corrupt police officer friends had been suspended. Powell had handed over the drugs and cash he discovered in the Inspector's bathroom but having been obtained illegally, it was useless as evidence in a court case. However, it was admissible in an internal police enquiry and their careers were at an end.

Powell also gave a statement about what he had seen late at night in the car park on the top of Ditchling Beacon but he couldn't say what was in the suitcase. Without additional evidence, they were unlikely to end up in court so Scott had been offered a deal to give evidence against them, in return for a lighter sentence but was so far saying nothing. Perhaps he still harboured hopes of escaping justice.

Powell had moved back into his house and was even happy to spend some time at the bar. He collected Afina from the airport and life was pretty much back to normal. Absence had definitely made the heart grow fonder, both for his bar and Afina.

Every so often, Powell thought about the kiss but tried not to dwell on the memory. He was looking forward to visiting Nottingham and taking Tina to dinner. He needed a distraction. If he could get through dinner with Tina without thinking about Afina, it would be revealing.

Powell believed the kiss had been the product of events as much as feelings. When he returned from Nottingham, he was going to look at holidays and keep his promise to Afina, to take her somewhere hot. Then perhaps their true feelings for each other would finally be resolved.

THE END

TRAFFICKING
Powell Book 1

Trafficking is big business and those involved show no remorse, have no mercy, only a deadly intent to protect their income.

Afina is a young Romanian girl with high expectations when she arrives in Brighton but she has been tricked and there is no job, only a life as a sex slave.

Facing a desperate future, Afina tries to escape and a young female police officer, who comes to her aid, is stabbed.

Powell's life has been torn apart for the second time and he is determined to find the man responsible for his daughter's death.

Action, violence and sex abound in this taut thriller about one of today's worst crimes.

5* Reviews

"This book is not for the faint hearted but it is a brilliant read."

"Keeps you at the edge of your seat throughout."

"Exciting, terrifying, brilliant."

"One of the best books I have read in a long time!"

"Will leave you breathless."

ABDUCTED
Powell Book 2

Powell returns in an action packed novel of violence, sex and betrayal!

He is trying to recover two children from Saudi Arabia, who have been abducted by their father.

In a culture where women are second class citizens, a woman holds the key to the success or failure of his mission.

Meanwhile, back in Brighton, Afina is trying to deal with a new threat from Romanian gangsters.

From the streets of Brighton to Riyadh, Powell must take the law into his own hands, to help the innocent.

5* Reviews

"Trafficking was masterful and this one is even better."

"Great thriller."

"Fabulous twists and turns."

"Strong, interesting characters."

DECEPTION
Powell Book 3

POWELL IS BACK IN A HEART POUNDING STORY THAT WILL LEAVE YOU BREATHLESS.

The Americans aren't happy with the changing political climate in Britain. Elements of the CIA and MI6 enter into a conspiracy to help shape the thinking of the British public.

Meanwhile ISIS has a plan to bring terror to the streets of Britain.

Powell is caught in the middle when he offers help to a former lover, whose life is in danger. Soon it becomes evident, someone will stop at nothing to see them both silenced.

Unsure who can be trusted, Powell must act to save the lives of his friends and right a terrible wrong.

5* Reviews

"Couldn't put the book down it was so gripping."

"Brilliant, like his other books, can't wait for his next book.."

"A thrill on every page."

REVENGE.

There is no greater motivator for evil than a huge sense of injustice!

Tom Ashdown, an unlikely hero, owns a betting shop in Brighton and gambles with his life when he stumbles across an attempted kidnapping, which leaves him entangled in a dangerous chain of events involving the IRA, a sister seeking revenge for the death of her brother and an informer in MI5 with a secret in his past.

Revenge is a fast paced thriller, with twists and turns at every step.

In a thrilling and violent climax everyone is intent on some form of revenge.

5* Reviews

"Fast paced from the start and it only goes faster!"

"This novel is a real page turner!"

"It will keep you on the edge of your seat."

"Revenge is an example of everything that I look for in an action thriller."

ENCRYPTION.

In a small software engineering company in England, a game changing algorithm for encrypting data has been invented, which will have far reaching consequences for the fight against terrorism.

The Security Services of the UK, USA and China all want to control the new software.

The Financial Director has been murdered and his widow turns to her brother-in-law to help discover the truth. But he soon finds himself framed for his brother's murder.

When the full force of government is brought to bear on one family, they seem to face impossible odds. Is it an abuse of power or does the end justify the means?

Only one man can find the answers but he is being hunted by the same people he once called friends and colleagues.

5* Reviews

"A Great English Spy Thriller."

"This is a great story! Once I started reading it, I could not put it down."

"Full of memorable characters and enough twists and turns to impress all diehard thriller junkies, it is a wonderful read"

"If you're a fan of Ludlum, and love descriptive prose like that of Michener, you'll be right at home."

ABOUT THE AUTHOR

Bill Ward lives in Brighton with his German partner Anja. He has retired from senior corporate roles in large IT companies and is now following a lifelong passion for writing! With 7 daughters, a son, stepson, 2 horses, a dog and 2 cats, life is always busy!

Bill's other great passion is supporting West Bromwich Albion, which he has been doing for more than 50 years!

Connect with Bill online:

Twitter: http://twitter.com/billward10bill

Facebook: http://facebook.com/billwardbooks